SECRET BEAST

AMELIA WILDE

CHAPTER ONE

Haley

THE HEATER IN my Toyota Camry blows snowflakes into the air.

I'm not a car person, but I'm pretty sure that's not supposed to happen. The saving grace of this situation is that I'm almost home from class. Fall semester is over. I'm one semester away from graduating with a degree in literature. And I won't have to drive to campus tomorrow getting tiny shards of frozen snow in my eyes.

The Camry huffs dutifully down the hill to our house, tucked as it is toward the back of Bishop's Landing. My headlights land on the front porch with its spinning wind chime that changes colors based on wind direction. The light swings over the patches of chipped siding and the dent in the garage from when my dad backed into the door a few years ago.

I'm home.

Bitter wind cuts through my coat on the run

from my car to the front door, shoulder bag banging against my hip. I need a different bag for next semester. One that can balance the weight of my laptop and books. The weight of my entire life right now. Some Constantines would just hire an assistant to solve this problem. We're not that kind of Constantine. If we were, we might also have skipped town to avoid the soul-crushing dark and cold.

Nothing, *nothing*, feels better than pulling open the door and stepping into warmth and light. After the frigid outdoors the air feels hot on my face.

My brother, Cash—all the Constantine good looks, none of the Constantine money—comes out of the kitchen with a big, steaming mug in his hands. "You're letting all the heat out."

He's wearing a cable-knit sweater and glower, which is…not like him. I make a show of shutting the door. He's usually pleasant. Easygoing. "Did something happen?"

When you have an inventor for a father, things happen. Sometimes, those things are whimsical color-changing wind chimes. Other times, they're chemical fires.

"The house is still standing," Cash says darkly. "He—"

"Haley, sweetheart, you're home." The warm delight in my father's voice crashes through Cash's bad mood. My dad appears at the door to his workshop, patting at his hair like he just woke up and discovered the rest of us are here. He hurries across the room, presses a kiss to my cheek. "Look at you. All these heavy things. Let me take your bag."

"I can get it, Dad." I don't stop him from taking the bag. These are the things that matter, in the end. A dad who loves you enough to help you out of your coat. He hangs it up on a hook by the door, a big smile on his face. "The heater in my car is broken, I think. Can you give me a ride back from Hal's tomorrow?"

"Sure, honey. Sure." His grin isn't proportional to my broken heater. He's happy, the kind of happy that only comes from an engineering breakthrough. "Did Cash tell you the good news?"

I throw a look at my brother, who scowls back at me over his mug. My dad doesn't seem to notice. "What's the good news?"

Dad's entire face brightens, throwing out several more megawatts of excitement. "You know I've been working on my energy project. A long time now, Hales. I've found an investor."

"Daddy, that's amazing." I throw my arms around him because screw Cash's bad mood. This is our dad, and he's happy. Even so. Worry pricks at the back of my mind. Even the less-rich Constantines know that you can't trust everyone who walks around with a checkbook. Even my absent-minded professor of a father knows that. Right? "Who is it? Is it official?"

"It's a Morelli." Cash has never sounded so flatly pissed.

My father's face falls and my heart drops with it. I turn my back on my brother, pulse pounding. "Dad, you know you can't work with the Morellis." The heat in the house closes in, but I'm glad for it. If we lost this heat, if we lost this house, I don't know what we'd do. "The Morellis are evil people. And more importantly, they hate Constantines."

Determination powers on in my dad's eyes. "They understand the vision, Haley. That's what matters. He understands what I'm trying to do."

"We can't, Daddy." I hate the way my voice rises to match the dull panic at the pit of my gut. "They could be trying to hurt you. I know how much the world needs your invention, but this is dangerous." My mind sputters to a halt, fried by a day of making nuanced arguments about literature and trying to tie up the semester's loose ends, and now my dad's terrible, reckless idea. "You can't do this."

"Don't worry, sweetheart." My father takes my face in his hands. "Everything will work out. I'll see you both after my meeting. Back in time for dinner."

"Eat with us before you go." I catch him by the sleeve. "We can talk about your pitch."

He winks at me. "I've already got it perfect, thanks to you. If I don't go now, I'll be late."

His coat is already going on over his shirt and tie and dress pants that haven't been ironed. My dad takes his keys from their hook with a flourish. I have the childish desire to tackle him somehow, to put my arms around his waist and keep him here, but I'm five foot two. I'm a hundred and ten pounds. That's not going to work. He's a grown man. A grown man with the power to ruin us.

He opens the door, letting in a gust of icy wind, and goes out with a dapper wave.

My shoulders sag. My soul sags. And I round on Cash. "Why did you let him meet with a Morelli? You were here all day."

"Don't come after me, Hales. I tried to warn him." Cash presses his lips into a thin, frustrated line. "He won't hear anything about it. I don't even think Petra could have convinced him."

Our oldest sister, Petra, would have had the best shot. She's reasonable. And patient. Now she lives with her husband and stays up late organizing charity events. She isn't home anymore, and neither was I. That's how this happened.

Guilt makes my throat ache. Guilt and worry. "I'm sorry. You couldn't have stopped him. I know that. What do we do now?"

"No idea." Cash watches me cross the room and fall onto the couch beside him. "I didn't know the phone calls were any different."

On a normal day, my dad's voice floats up from the workshop for hours. Making connections, he calls it. He starts every call by saying, *this is Phillip Constantine, and I want to change the world.* He's a well-meaning engineer who tries so hard it kills me. The relief I felt at completing another semester is gone, replaced by dread. "Did he say which Morelli he was meeting?"

"No. He just raved about the guy. Apparently he's found the only honorable, whip-smart Morelli on the planet. Focused." Cash mimics Dad's voice. "He's *focused*."

"Focused on hating us." That's what the Morellis do. They hate our family. They poke and prod and insult our family. There is no earthly way that a Morelli genuinely wants to help my dad get his invention into people's hands across the world. They're more likely to steal it, or starve it of money. Either way, the work would die with them. My dad's dream would die.

Cash doesn't say anything to that. How am I supposed to cook now? How am I supposed to root through the fridge and put something on the stove and chat with Cash while he sets the table? We'd both have to pretend our dad isn't taking the biggest risk of his life. I can't do it.

My stomach clenches.

Living the way we do is already a risk. In general, our family doesn't tolerate outliers, like our cousin Elaine. Behind the shimmering facade of the Constantine lifestyle there are sharp edges underneath. The claws come out if you step out of line, and my dad has been out of line for years. Our house is too small. It's not in a prestigious area of Bishop's Landing. We don't have maintenance staff. No maids, no gardeners. When we were younger, my dad's brother would argue with him about it in cultured Constantine tones that cut to the quick.

I heard the things he said. *Disgrace. Embarrassment. Barely a Constantine.*

All because we don't care about flashy things

and real estate.

What would they do if they found out he's aligned himself with a Morelli? I rub my palms over my jeans. It's too soon to get lost in anxiety about our family's reaction to this Morelli investor. This *possible* investor. This is only the first meeting, I hope, and my dad wouldn't sign anything without talking it through first. I'm sure he wouldn't.

A knock sounds at the door. I leap up from the couch to answer it. Oh, sweet relief. "He changed his mind," I tell Cash. "You have to help me this time. Convince him to stay. If we can get him to stay for dinner—"

The rest of the sentence dies an early death.

"Hello, Haley." Caroline Constantine is a vision in winter white, her blonde hair pulled back into a flawless chignon and her cheeks a delicate pink from the cold. My aunt doesn't belong on our porch in her snow-colored Prada coat. It's the kind of coat you wear when you're going to be driven from place to place, not tromping through slush. Caroline's black town car waits behind mine in the driveway, the engine idling.

"Please, come in." I'm a beat too late, and the corners of Caroline's mouth turn down. Not enough that she's actually frowning. Just enough that I know these aren't the Constantine graces she expects. Her eyes flick over the overflowing bookshelves in the living room and Cash's scattered homework on the table. I shut the door behind her. "Would you like something to drink? Hot tea?"

"Aunt Caroline." Cash rises from his seat and comes over to us. He kisses Caroline's cheek, and she softens at his charm. She's always liked Cash the best of my siblings. I think he reminds her of her sons. "What brings you to the house?"

"No, thank you, Haley." Caroline fixes her gaze on Cash. "I thought I'd stop by and see how my brother-in-law is getting along. He hasn't been present at any of the family gatherings lately."

Cash and I—and sometimes our sister, Petra—are the ones who represent our tiny branch of the family at Caroline's parties. My dad can't be bothered to go. What's the point of being seen at a party when you could be working on your next world-changing invention?

"He's been hard at work lately," Cash supplies, an indulgent smile on his face. "You know how he is. He's going to change the world with his innovations in wind energy."

"So he'll be working on it now, then." Caroline pulls off one of her white gloves, then the other, and tucks them both into her purse. "I'll go speak with him in his workshop."

"He's not down there." I'm too quick with it, too desperate, and Caroline notices. She raises her eyebrows and I rearrange my expression into something sheepish and apologetic. "The heater in my car broke."

She narrows her eyes. "Isn't your car the one parked in front of mine?" There's tacit disapproval in her question. It's not seemly to keep your car parked in the driveway like a poor person who doesn't have room in their garage. It's not seemly to have a ten-year-old car with a broken heater, either. Constantines drive Bentleys and Porches, not Toyota Camrys.

"He went to speak to our mechanic." Cash laughs a little, as if meeting with a mechanic is one of Dad's many lovable quirks. As if he ever meets with mechanics. "See if it was something he could fix here at home. You know he loves tinkering with engines."

I hold my breath and pray that Caroline Constantine doesn't know that most mechanics in the area close at five, and it's too late for my dad to have gone there. I send up a secondary prayer that she hasn't found out through her extensive network about Dad talking to a Morelli in the first place.

Caroline has the power to make anyone's life difficult in Bishop's Landing, and since her husband died—my dad's brother—she's been twice as stringent about keeping the family image polished. That's what this is: a visit to keep us in line. Not a friendly chat.

She's a beautiful woman, but not entirely real. It's like she's been carved out of ice. "You're graduating in the spring, isn't that right, Haley?"

"Yes, I am. My degree will be in English literature. There are tons of opportunities that—"

"You'll need to make a name for yourself." Caroline looks me in the eye. God, I wish I was in some kind of Constantine armor and not skinny jeans with a tunic top that's cute and convenient for walking from class to class. I look like the opposite of a Constantine princess. The opposite of what Caroline wants. "You'll be representing our family, and it is crucial that we maintain our reputation."

"Oh, of course." I put on a smile that she doesn't exactly return. "I'm hoping to get a position somewhere in the city, and then in a few years—"

"You'll run it by me first. Approved companies only. Approved positions only." Her tone softens. "I only want the best for you."

"Thank you." *Wanting the best,* coming from her, is a threat. My voice is rising again and I struggle to bring it back down. "That will be so helpful."

"We can all be helpful to each other, I think." Caroline looks me in the eye, then Cash, then takes a step back so she can survey us both. "The two of you are adults. It's time you impressed upon your father that he is a member of this family, and members of this family do their part."

"We'll talk to him, won't we, Hales?" Cash winks at me, and I latch on to that wink like a lifeline. My dad doesn't care about money. He doesn't care about prestige. He cares about changing the world with his inventions.

Caroline could stop him from doing all that. A few well-placed words from her, and no investor in the country will work with him. I underestimated her. I underestimated how much it would matter if my dad wanted to spend his time working instead of socializing at the Constantine compound. I can't let her crush him. Not the man who read to me every night before I fell asleep. The man who let me stand on a workbench next to him while he sketched out his latest invention. The man who hung my coat up for me not even an hour ago.

"We'll talk to him tonight." I put on my biggest, bravest smile. It's directly proportional to my terror. I can't let my father sign that deal. Whatever happens. "As soon as he gets home. Did you want to wait for him, Aunt Caroline, or—"

"No." She tugs one elegant glove up to her wrist, then the other. "I have things to attend to this evening." She leans across and kisses my cheek, then steps in to do the same for Cash. "Behave yourselves, you two. And give your father my best."

CHAPTER TWO

Haley

D AD'S NOT HOME for dinner.
I put off cooking, hoping he'll walk in the door with a bag of takeout.

"You have to stop going in there," Cash calls from the living room to where I'm standing in the kitchen, staring into the sink like it'll give me a plan for putting food on the table when anything could be happening to our father. "He's not going to magically appear."

I pace back out to the living room and check the driveway for signs of an approaching car. Nothing. "We have to do something."

"There's nothing to do." Cash rubs both hands over his hair and sags back against the couch, neck cushioned by tensed arms. "Not until he comes home. Unless you want to attack the Morelli family. If we start a war, maybe no one will wonder what Dad was doing."

"I'm not saying we attack them." We don't

have a lot of options for doing that, anyway. A bunch of kitchen knives and some half-finished inventions. I have a wild, ridiculous vision of charging at them with the color-changing wind chime. "I'm saying we do something other than sitting here."

"You haven't been sitting," Cash points out. "You've been walking back and forth from here to the kitchen for two hours." He's not even pretending to look at his laptop. I've been pacing, but Cash has been holding his empty coffee cup for the better part of forty-five minutes. "He'll come back."

"I don't think he will." I'm headed for the stairs to his workshop before I realize what I'm doing. Footsteps come along behind me.

"What are you looking for?"

"He had to write down the address. He wouldn't have remembered it otherwise." The workshop is a long, wide space, with workbenches along the back wall. Lights attached to moving bits of metal and plastic give the space a dim glow. I find the light switch without looking. Dad replaced the fluorescent bulbs with special ones that are meant to mimic sunlight. He claims this means he can work longer hours without missing the benefits of being outside.

I push away the morbid thought that he might never be inside our home again and concentrate on the notepads.

Yellow legal pads. White scratch pads. One from the grocery store that they gave out last Valentine's Day. Most of these are piled up near Dad's computer, wedged into a corner of the workbench. Pages on pages of notes.

And on top of all the notepads—his phone. My shoulders drop.

"What is it?" Cash asks.

"Dad's phone." I pick it up and hold it high so he can see it. "He left it here. We can't even call him. What if he stalled somewhere? What if he's stranded on the side of the road?"

I take a deep breath and swipe across the screen. No passcode, because he'd forget what it was and lock himself out. My dad has had this old iPhone for close to four years now. That is the equivalent of a cell-phone century and I'm seized with a panic that it will die in my hands and I'll never find out what happened to him. It's slow, this phone, slow to respond to my touch.

The calendar app takes forever to load. When it does, I can see that it's blank. I curse under my breath.

Cash comes to look over my shoulder. "Notes

app?"

"Maybe."

It's right there in the first note. An address in New York City. Under that is the name of the person he's meeting.

Leo Morelli.

Oh, god.

Cash's face has gone pale. "He didn't say that's who it was." His defensive tone gives me another pang of guilt. I shouldn't have blamed him for this earlier. Shouldn't have even suggested that. "He never gave me the name."

My heart knocks against my sternum, pulse pounding in my temples. "Okay. I'm going after him."

I take the stairs two at a time, Cash chasing after me. "Hales, you can't go. It's the Morellis. It's Leo."

Everyone in Bishop's Landing and probably all of New York City knows who Leo Morelli is. He's the Beast of Bishop's Landing. That's what everyone calls him. His older brother, Lucian, is evil in the way of all Morellis, but Leo is more unpredictable. More dangerous.

He likes to make life hard for people in our family.

He's good at it.

There isn't really a *good* Morelli in this situation, but Leo's the worst of the entire family. "I don't care which one of them it is. He shouldn't be there alone."

"We shouldn't be there, either."

"You're not coming."

"I'm not letting you go by yourself."

I round on him while I pull my coat over my shoulders. "I'm going, Cash, and you're staying here in case Dad's already on his way home."

Cash steps around me and blocks the door. "I know this is going to sound crazy, but what if we called Caroline? He might be in trouble. She could help."

"We're not calling any of them." Involving the larger Constantine family would be a mistake. A fatal error. Caroline doesn't allow mistakes. And my father talking to a Morelli would be a mistake. A big one. She could probably figure out where he's gone. Hell, she probably has contacts that can track cell phones, but if she got involved, she wouldn't help. More likely she would leave him to the wolves for the sin of failing the Constantine name.

My brother's face is red and gets redder. "You don't know what you're walking into."

Hat. Mittens. Keys. I shove my wallet into the

pocket of my coat. "Stay here and wait for Dad to get home. Call me if he does. Otherwise I'll bring him home with me."

I reach for the doorknob and Cash catches me by the elbow. He turns me back around and crushes me in a hug. Cash has been taller than me for years, and stronger. He's still my little brother. I squeeze him back and pull my hat back into place.

"I'll come back." Unlike my father, I don't give him a timeline.

"If anything happens..." Cash's eyes burn into mine. "If *anything* happens—"

"I'll call you."

"I'll kill them."

"I know." I put a hand on his shoulder. He's trembling. So am I. This is bad. Our family has weathered catastrophes, but something like this can spiral out of control. "Have something to eat. We'll both be home soon."

My Toyota hums to life in the driveway and releases a breath of glittering snowflakes into my face. I crank the heat anyway. Maybe it will find its courage again. If it doesn't, then I'll freeze my ass off to save my dad.

I hope that's the worst of it.

The route to the highway takes me through

the heart of Bishop's Landing, a town filled with mansions. The Constantines live here. The *other* Constantines. I feel like I have this last name by accident. There are people out in the world with blonde hair and blue eyes who never have their aunt Caroline show up at the front door with a disapproving expression and barbed comments. I'm as far removed from them as I am the real Constantines—the ones who live in the gorgeous estates I'm driving past now.

The Morellis live in Bishop's Landing, too.

So why is Leo Morelli meeting my father in New York City?

Once I've merged onto the highway I tug the mittens halfway off so I can have a better grip on the wheel while keeping my fingers from going numb. I drive five over the speed limit all the way into the city, my phone's GPS steering me to the address my dad left.

With every block that passes, my heart sinks lower. Acid burns at the back of my tongue. This area isn't good. The streetlights are few and far between, and I drive past more than one with only remnants of shattered glass.

"The destination is on your left," my phone announces.

I pull the car over and peer at the building. A

boarded-up shop on the first floor, graffiti on the boards. One of them has a torn-off corner as if something chewed into the wood. The rest of the block isn't any better. I'm parked next to the curb, and beyond that is a crumbling sidewalk. It's not livable here. Industrial, really, with a wharf jutting out into the river.

No sign of my dad.

I'm not going to be able to find him sitting in the car, so I pull my mittens up, put my phone in my pocket, and step out onto the street.

Voices from a nearby alley echo across the deserted block. Most of the river is covered in ice, but some of it is free to slap against the pilings. It's colder by the water. I would give anything for a warm car to drive away in.

I would give even more for my dad to be here, too.

The voices from the alley rise. Laughter. Hardened laughter. The Morellis wouldn't hold an actual meeting in a place like this. They would lure a man into a trap. There's no time to call Cash and ask him if he can drive to the city. No time to do anything but check the alley myself. Stay out of sight. If my dad is there, I'll get him out somehow.

He might be hurt. Bleeding. I have to help

him.

An icy spike of wind wriggles down the collar of my coat as I hurry toward the opening of the alley. Light flickers there, spilling out onto the sidewalk. I get as close as I dare. One, two, three. I stick my head around the corner of the building.

Six guys. No, eight. Maybe ten. Homeless, possibly, by the looks of them. Some of them have heavy coats. Almost all of them have hats. One guy has makeshift gloves made from plastic bags. Their faces glow in the light of a fire they've made in a barrel. They huddle in close, shifting positions to take turns warming their hands.

None of them is my dad.

Shit.

"Come here, girl. You aren't from around here, are you?"

I pull my head out of sight, fear skittering up my arms and drawing my shoulders up, up, up. I'm three steps down the street when they catch up.

"Where are you going in such a hurry?" I regret not running. I thought walking would make them less likely to chase me. It was foolish, and now there's one man on either side of me and my car is across the street.

"I have to get home."

"We saw you looking at us," one says. He's the man with plastic bags on his hands, and he strips them off and lets them fall to the ground. "We want to see you, too."

The other man takes a sudden step toward me and I react on instinct, going the other way. Toward the building. My shoulder hits the brick and I turn so the wall is against my back. Trapped. I'm trapped against rough brick, and now three of them are blocking the path to my car.

"I'm leaving." I'm proud of how level my voice sounds. "Get out of my way."

"You came to our party." The third man presses in and reaches for me. I slap at his arm but he laughs. "It's probably because you're bored at home, aren't you? Wanted some fun tonight. Let's show her a good time."

I try to edge sideways, but one of them puts a foot out and angles his body to stop me. More hands reach in. Too many to swipe away. One paws at the waist of my coat. Someone's dirty fingers are on my chin. I'm going to be sick. I'm going to pass out. Those two things aren't options for me right now, because if I do either thing, they'll take advantage of that weakness.

If they get me onto the ground...

If they get my coat off…

A blind punch at one of the men. It's useless. I'm wearing mittens. He laughs and grabs my hand. No—the mitten itself. It comes off in a hard tug and tears sting the corners of my eyes.

A strong voice breaks through the clamor. "Find somewhere else to play."

The guy with my mitten turns around, a sneer on his face. His confidence closes off like a shutter over a window. "Guys." He tenses, voice rising. "Guys, guys." My mitten flutters to the sidewalk. The man who held it is already gone, leaving his friends abandoned.

One of them is reaching into my pocket when the hand appears on his shoulder.

A big hand. A male one. The hand pulls him back like he's nothing and the man's face contorts, his head crumpling toward his shoulder. "Oh, fuck," he breathes, and then he's lurching away. He's free because a man in black—tall and dark-haired and dark-eyed—ignores him as he steps neatly into the open space left behind.

This close, he is all intensity and movement. Practiced. Controlled.

It looks easy for him to bring back his fist and drive it into another man's nose. To catch that man when he starts to fall and send a cracking blow into the side of his cheek.

He drops the man unceremoniously, the way you'd drop a dirty dishrag into the laundry, and kicks at the groaning body at his feet.

"Go on," he snaps, like he's talking to a feral dog. Less than a feral dog.

He kicks the guy again and he rolls over onto hands and knees. He's halfway to his feet when my white knight plants a foot in the middle of his back and sends him spiraling onto the bare concrete. He must be off-balance from the blows, because his forehead meets the sidewalk with a dull thud. It has to hurt.

Adrenaline spirals down through my veins and lights up my fingertips. The air is so cold, so clear. I can feel the heat from the fire in the drum. I can taste it.

He saved me.

He saved me from whatever those men were going to do, and he hurt them. He hurt them because he could.

We watch the man get unsteadily to his feet and stumble toward the alley. More faces appear around the corner, eyes wide. A few people hurry out from the alley and go the opposite direction, fading into the gloom. They don't want to be here if this man is around.

This man, in his beautiful black overcoat. He looks like a photo from a men's fashion magazine, only sharper. Even in profile, the lines of his face make my chest ache.

His face…

It's familiar somehow.

My mind is a mess, tangled up in the dread and relief of this near-miss, and I can't place him until he turns to look at me with eyes like midnight. My heart stutters. I'm from a family known for its beauty, but I have never seen a person so agonizingly gorgeous.

Recognition makes my breath catch. Leo Morelli.

I've only seen him in glossy photographs in local magazines and online gossip blogs. On paper he's handsome in a vague movie star way. In person he's breathtaking.

I try to take a step back, but I'm against the wall.

There's nowhere to run from the Beast of Bishop's Landing.

CHAPTER THREE

Haley

LEO MORELLI IS a thousand times more intimidating in person than the men he just chased away.

My dad was right. He is focused. He's unbearably focused. His eyes linger on my face, then slip lower. He returns his gaze to mine with a sneer.

It's outrageously unfair that he's so beautiful with that expression on his face.

"Look at you, with your pale blonde hair and porcelain skin and that willowy body." My peacoat might as well be nothing under his knowing dark eyes. "I'd pick you out of a lineup in a second. A Constantine. I'm right, aren't I?"

He steps closer. I press my back harder against the bricks, bracing for him to touch me. To kill me, even. That's what Morellis do. They hurt people. They kill people. Cash was right. I never should have come here on my own. Leo blocks out the rest of the street. His face could be the last thing I see before I die.

No. I'm not going to die. I came here for a reason.

He cocks his head to the side, the movement graceful. Almost elegant. "What's a pretty Constantine like you doing in a neighborhood like this? You're not Elaine, so you didn't come here for a hit. No, you must be here for something else. *Someone* else." Another slow smile.

"I came here to save my father." I stand up straight. Peel my hands off the wall. "Save him from you."

A laugh so dark it matches his eyes. "Daddy can't take care of himself? I should have known. The Constantine men need their daughters to protect them. You must be the one he talked about tonight. *Haley.*"

My body is one huge heartbeat, my thoughts and bones and skin reduced to the drum of the pulse in my ears. "Where is he? What have you done with him?"

"Don't worry, darling." *Darling* sends an electric cold tiptoeing down my spine and it's all I can do not to shiver. The sound of that word in his mouth... "He's getting everything he ever wanted."

"Don't play with him."

"Play with him?" Leo smiles at me, mocking. "I would never. He'll have his invention made. It will change the world. And the Morellis will get richer. I wonder what Caroline Constantine will think about that."

Caroline can never find out what my dad has done, because she'll go ballistic in the Constantine sense, which is more dignified than when the Morellis target someone—but just as deadly. Leo has already been toying with the Constantines. With Winston, especially, and that means he knows all about Caroline, too. He wouldn't hesitate to reveal this to her. He would do it in the most mortifying way possible. That would be the end for us.

Caroline and all the rest of the Constantines have always rejected my dad's ideas, but he can't become a traitor to the family. They would expel him. Blacklist us. They might do worse. Appearances are everything in the Constantine family. Caroline would do anything to protect the image.

Anything would come in the form of a tragic accident or an undiscovered allergy or sad twist of fate that no one could have predicted. Caroline will keep her hands clean. No one would ever know, except me and Cash.

I've backed up into the wall again, but I find my voice. "No. Please. Caroline doesn't need to be involved. Just release him from the agreement."

An amused laugh. "Why would I do that when I stand to make a fortune?"

The laugh doesn't warm his features. Faint sparks play in the dark center of his eyes—shards of moonlight, caught in a black sky. That moonlight is never going to get free again. This is how the conversation ends. This is how it all ends, unless I do something right now.

I don't have anything to offer. No trust fund. No limitless credit card. We're the only Constantines who have no hope of matching the Morellis dollar for dollar. All I have in my coat pocket is my phone and a pass for the campus bus route.

I'm the only thing I've got.

"You like to make deals." Everybody knows that about Leo and his brother. They're heavily into real estate, both in the city and in Bishop's Landing. They like to buy and sell buildings as a cover for all the real antagonism they do. The real evil, like tricking my father into a business deal, knowing that he's not like the other Constantines. "Trades. What would you take in trade?"

His eyes move down over my face. To the collar of my coat. His slow perusal burns through the cold and my coat and even the clothes underneath. I hold my breath, like he'll look away if I'm a statue.

Leo does not look away. He trails his gaze back up the front of me, over the button that holds the coat closed over my breasts, and his eyes land at the exposed hollow of my throat. I should have worn a scarf. I should have brought Cash. I should have brought all the Constantine firepower and hired security and I didn't. It's too late. It's way too late.

My face heats. He can tell, I'm sure of it. He can tell that if he stripped away the coat and the clothes, he would find an innocent virgin underneath.

He knows because it's true. Men like Leo Morelli always know. He would take that innocence and do things to me that I haven't dared to dream about, that I've held my mind away from because thinking about those things is an endless descent into a dark night. There's no coming back. There's no staying the same, when you think about hands like his and a mouth like his and eyes like his—

Eyes that catch mine. He's done with his assessment and I remember, suddenly, painfully, that I asked him to trade with me. The next move is his.

"I might be willing to make a trade."

My knees give out, and I'm glad for the wall. I hook a hand around the nearest brick and keep myself standing. "You'll let him go?"

"I'll consider it."

He takes a step toward me and stops, bending to pick something up off the sidewalk.

It's my mitten.

Leo holds it out to me with a sarcastic flourish, the wrist hole pulled open by his fingers. It feels like a trap, sticking my hand into my own mitten.

I can't do it.

He makes an impatient noise and pushes it over my hand himself. "Helpless, pathetic Constantines," he says. "Like father, like daughter. Come with me."

All the breath goes out of me. I summon enough oxygen to speak—barely. "Right now?"

The look Leo gives me is so cutting I want to cover my face with my hands. "You could stay here. Keep showing your tits to every fuckface who walks by."

I jerk away from the wall like it's the brick that stung me and not his words. Crossing my arms over my chest is a pointless move, but I do it anyway, face hot and red. I'm wearing a winter coat. I wasn't showing anyone my tits. The fact that I was arched back against a wall in front of Leo Morelli should be incidental.

A gust of wind knifes under my collar. "Where are you taking me?"

"Do you see your gullible father here?" He brims with irritation and I have the ridiculous thought that it's my fault we're out here. It's not. It's this monster's fault and no one else's. "You want to see him, you'll be a good girl and come with me."

I could die. I could die, but instead I take the first step and follow him back down the block. He turns at an alley, an empty twin of the one with the barrel and the fire and those men. And there, in the alley, is my dad's car. He's not in it.

Leo holds up a hand to stop me from asking where my dad is and opens a door set into the side of the building. Fear makes my stomach clench. He could be luring me, too. He could be opening the door to a life where I'm too late, too late, too late.

But there's no lifeless body on the other side. No cruel trick. It's a restaurant, or some very small private club. Wine-colored tablecloths. Sturdy furniture.

Behind the bar, a large screen showing various shots of black-and-white alleyways. There you can see my dad's car. My car. The vagrants huddled around the barrel.

Leo Morelli saw me coming. He knew I'd be there.

Dad sits in view of the door. When he sees me, he gives me an excited wave. A stack of papers waits on the table in front of him, a pen thrown to the side. They've already signed.

Leo's voice is close, his breath warm on the shell of my ear. I can't take my eyes off my father. Can't help but see the way his eyes go from me to Leo, who must be a terrifying shadow in the dark of the alley. "If you want to save your father, you'll have to pay," he says, and my toes curl. There's a whisper of pressure at my pocket. "Meet me here in twenty-four hours."

CHAPTER FOUR

Haley

I'M TOO AFRAID to let my dad out of my sight, and shaking too badly to drive. The Camry gets abandoned by the curb. It's a long, quiet ride back to Bishop's Landing.

I can't say anything. Can't begin to put into words what my father has done by signing those papers. By going to that meeting at all. We could have died. I narrowly avoided a fate worse than death. I still might die. There's a business card with an address scrawled across it in my pocket. I'm afraid to take it out. I don't want to show my father. I barely even want to acknowledge it to myself. Leo Morelli wants me to meet him in twenty-four hours. What will he do to me?

We're wending our way through the ritzy neighborhoods when my father sighs. "It's only a business deal, Haley. You don't have to look so upset."

My fingernails dig into the fabric of my purse

in spite of myself. "Dad, you signed a contract with Leo Morelli." I hold up the copy that Leo so helpfully provided to my father. Dad signed both of the documents. "This says he owns the rights to your invention forever. In every country, in every possible jurisdiction. He can put his name on it, if he wants. Call it his. It *is* his."

"Not so bad as that. There are provisions for me. And every country will see my work."

I can't get through to him. He signed this, and I'm going to have to get him out of it.

There's no one else. Petra's married and busy. Cash is nineteen. So far, only the three of us—and Leo Morelli—know about the deal. The fewer the better. Caroline can't find out. My thoughts come in staccato bursts that collide with each other and start breaking down as we pull into the driveway. I'm the first out of the car, taking huge breaths of the crystal clear air.

The front door of the house bursts open. "Dad?" Cash sounds frantic, panicked. Every minute must have eaten at him, if he can't put on his usual level-headed image.

"It's both of us," I call. The wind bites through my coat. "My car is in the city. I'm going to have to hire a tow truck." Dad climbs out of the driver's seat.

"I hope you didn't wait for me to eat." He heads for the door like this night was a speed bump and not a train wreck.

"Eat?" Cash's eyes are wide and white in the spill of light from the door. "Nobody could eat. We thought—" He looks away. Can't bring himself to say what he thought might happen.

Inside, I take off my coat but the heat refuses to get close. A chill has settled over my skin that I can't shake. "He signed the papers," I tell Cash, and myself.

Cash groans, despair edging his voice. "Dad, you didn't. Tell me you didn't fucking sign anything with a Morelli sitting across the table."

"He understands the vision." Dad's face darkens, eyebrows pulling together. "Nothing untoward happened at the meeting."

"Dad." It's all I can do to keep my voice level. I'd rather scream. "You signed an agreement with Leo Morelli. He's going to take everything you have. For all I know, he owns your invention now, and you don't have the rights. You didn't take a lawyer with you. You didn't have anyone review the documents. You—" I'm going to cry. If I let a single tear fall, I won't be able to stop. The contract could have contained anything, and my dad was too enamored with the idea to see. "It was a bad deal. Whatever he said, it was a bad deal."

Watching him understand what I'm saying is more painful than watching him walk out the door for the meeting. My dad's face falls, shoulders sagging, and his hands go up to his hair. "We don't know that. We don't know it was underhanded. There's no reason to believe—"

"There's every reason," Cash shouts, and our father flinches at the sound. Dad only ever raises his voice to be heard above a particularly noisy invention, and now his only son looks ready to punch him. Cash's fists open and close at his sides. "There's every reason to believe they fucked you over. You sat down with a Morelli. I can't—" A sharp laugh. "I can't believe you're standing here right now. The Morellis kill people. That's what they do."

"You don't know that."

"I do know that. And I know the contract is terrible."

"I can renegotiate." Dad's voice shakes. "He'll understand. He's…"

The rest of the sentence fades away. There's nothing he can say to paint Leo Morelli as a hero. Leo didn't offer my father a contract out of the goodness of his heart, and he didn't save me from those men out of some moral obligation. He did it because he wanted to use us both. That's what he does.

Headlights sweep across the living room and all of us freeze. My heart climbs up into my throat. I want to believe Leo didn't follow us here, but there are no limits to what he'll do. Everyone knows that.

I'm already walking to the door to meet him when the knock sounds. "I'm coming," I say automatically, though if it's Leo on the other side, then I've wasted my manners.

I open the door.

It's not him.

Richard Joseph, Jr. stands on the front porch, breath crystallizing in the air, an enormous bouquet of flowers in his hands.

"Hey, Haley." He's a smooth one, Rick. His hair is a shade too dark to be a real Constantine, but he wants to be one. He wants to be part of Aunt Caroline's family so much that he's willing to overlook the small fact that we're barely Constantines at all. We're only Constantines when we're embarrassing her. "For you."

I take the flowers and step back to let him in. It's only after he's across the threshold that I come to my senses. Dad paces the living room, tugging at his hair, and Cash glares at the fireplace.

"Mr. Constantine," Rick booms, and Dad throws a distracted glance at him. "Any plans for the weekend?"

"No. No. I'll be working. I have some new ideas that could be useful."

"I'm sure you do." Dad is too busy hurrying for the steps to the workshop to see Rick's sneer. As rich and smart as Rick is, he can't control his own face when it counts. He's a beat behind in turning the sneer back into an approving smile for my benefit, but it's back in place when he turns his green eyes on me. "What about you, doll?"

"She's busy." Cash crosses his arms over his chest.

Rick laughs. "I don't think you answer for her, buddy."

If nothing else, being in this family has graced me with the ability to smile sadly at Rick while my brother bristles and my dad hides in his workshop.

"I am a little busy," I admit. "We're working some things out with one of my father's recent inventions."

Rick's laugh is appropriate for a hilarious joke. "Oh, yeah? Did Caroline finally take pity and offer him some financing?"

"No," I say, my voice breaking on the word. I shouldn't share anything with Rick. We're not close, but my emotions are too near the surface. Leo Morelli tore down all my defenses, and I've had no time to rebuild them.

His expression morphs into wariness. "What's wrong?"

He seems sincere in the moment, and I'm so close to crumbling. "Nothing."

"Haley."

I shake my head, lips trembling. A tear falls down my cheek. Twenty-four hours. What's going to happen to me in twenty-four hours? "Oh God, Rick. It's so terrible."

A sob breaks from me. It's my brother who answers in a grim tone. "It's the Morellis. That's his new fucking investor. Leo."

The concern drops from Rick's face like a discarded mask. "Don't even joke about that."

"He's not joking," I say on a shuddery breath.

Rick's skin turns pale. Almost as pale as mine. "You know why Caroline keeps that bulldog around? What's his name—Ronan? Not for the Morellis. For traitors."

The pit of my gut turns to solid ice. He's right. I don't have twenty-four hours to solve this problem. Twenty-four hours is long enough for

Leo Morelli to wreak havoc on my essentially defenseless father. Twenty minutes is long enough.

And Caroline won't need that much time to send Ronan after us.

We're going to die. If I wait, we're going to die.

Arriving on Leo's doorstep early won't guarantee our survival, but it will give us a chance. I pretend to be very taken with the flowers. "Oh, I know." I shake my head, wiping away my tears. "You know how Dad is. It's a shiny idea, and he'll forget after an hour in his workshop."

Rick frowns. "Then why are you crying?"

"That time of the month," I say, forcing a smile.

Rick's expression eases. His entire adulthood has been about getting in with the Constantines, hence this Friday-night visit. It was a gamble in the first place, coming here for me when he could be trying to get closer to Winston or Elaine. The last thing he needs is guilt by association. "You sure about that?"

I take a deep breath. Every second that passes is as loud as a tolling bell. "Listen. I need a ride somewhere."

Here's my gamble. Here's my roll of the dice.

I'm betting that Rick knows about the Morellis almost as well as he knows about the Constantines. That's one surefire way to be in the in-crowd—to have information that other people want.

A pleased smile. "To dinner?"

"Wait here." I push the flowers into his hands. "Choose a nice place for those. Please?"

It's not kind, what I'm doing. I know that. My hands tremble while I go through my closet. I have a limited wardrobe compared to Caroline's daughters, but it's not a problem I can solve right now. The dress that comes to hand is black and sexy. The sexiest one I have. That's what Leo Morelli will demand. I can't show up in leggings and a hoodie and expect to trade myself for my father's life.

I spend ten minutes in front of the mirror, covering cheeks that are rosy and hot from the biting cold and Leo Morelli's searing eyes. Shoes. A purse that matches.

This feels like a moment for red lipstick. I don't own any. So I settle for the one shade I do have. It's called Insist. Fitting.

The last thing I do is write a note. I skip the names like a coward.

Please don't worry about me—I'm heading

*out to smooth things over. Back before you
know it. Love you both, Haley*

Rick whistles at me as I make my way down
the stairs. "Any restaurant you want, doll. I'll call
in a favor."

His car idles in the driveway, waiting for us.
Rick helps me in. Guilt and anxiety make my
heart feel too big for my rib cage. It doesn't have
enough room to beat, and it hurts when it does. I
wish I could have hugged them goodbye, but
Cash would have stopped me. I know he would
have. He'd have put himself between me and the
door.

Rick pulls out of the driveway, brimming with
excitement. "I meant what I said. Name the
place."

It's warm in the car, but I'm frozen. "How
much do you know about Leo Morelli?"

His hands tighten on the steering wheel. "I
know your father should stay away from him.
Cancel any meetings he might have taken."

"I need a ride."

"I can't take you to Leo Morelli. Damn it,
Haley, you know better—"

I shove my hand into my pocket and come up
with the piece of paper. It only takes a few
seconds to read, and then it doesn't matter if Rick

takes the paper or tries to stop me. "You don't have to take me to him. Just to my car. My dad signed a contract, Rick. I have to get him out of it."

I let this hang in the air. Rick comes to a stop at the first intersection after our house, hand hovering over the turn signal. If Caroline finds out he helped me, then he's going to lose all his access to the Constantine family. Maybe worse, given the existence of Ronan. So he shouldn't help. But if he does, then I'll owe him a favor. The struggle writes itself across his face. Either way, he could end up as screwed as the rest of us. Ah, the joys of being a Constantine.

"I can't do it." His shoulders tighten.

"You have to."

"Your father will know. Your brother saw you leave with me."

"We had a late dinner, and you dropped me off at my car." I sound so much more confident than I feel. Part of me wishes Rick would insist on dinner and take the choice out of my hands, but that's not how these things work. My dad's name is signed in ink. It could be signed in blood. What kind of daughter would let that happen? "That's all. I need a ride to my car and an address."

Rick curses under his breath. He wants to

drive into Bishop's Landing. He wants to take me to a restaurant where we can see and be seen, and he can get one step closer to an official place in the Constantine family.

He turns toward New York City instead.

CHAPTER FIVE

Leo

THE KNOCK AT the door to my den is purposefully soft. "Are you awake, sir?"

"Do I look asleep to you?"

"No." Gerard, my head of security and the general manager of my life, steps into the room. I have no idea how long I've been sitting here. A glance at the clock tells me it's been two hours. "Your sister is here."

"Which sister?"

"Eva, Mr. Morelli."

I toss the book I've been not-reading onto the side table. "If you left her standing by the door—"

"He didn't, Leo. Don't be mean." Eva comes into the room, pulling her gloves off one by one. Gerard takes her coat, and the two of them exchange a look that makes me want to fire him on the spot. I don't give in to the urge. He's too good at his job, and finding people who won't spy for my eldest brother, Lucian, is a bigger task than one might think. In the five years he's been with me, Gerard hasn't fucked me over once. I let the Constantines think Trenton Alto, Lucian's man, is the one who's closest to me.

I let the Constantines think lots of ridiculous things.

"Diet Coke?" Gerard asks.

"Yes, thank you. Hi." Eva bends down next to my chair and kisses my cheek, then settles herself on the long sofa across from my chair. "I heard some news about you."

I wait until Gerard is gone to answer her. Not because I don't trust him—I have to, if I'm going to have him in my house most of the time—but because it's obnoxious as fuck to have to leave mid-conversation. Gerard would never admit that. "You have to stop talking to your friends about how handsome and irresistible I am. It's fucked up to entertain conversations about your own brother like that."

"Not that kind of news." Gerard appears with a can of Diet Coke, which he presents to Eva. She cracks it open and takes a long drink. "I heard you started a new venture to fuck around with the Constantines."

"I wouldn't call that a new venture. More like old money."

She snorts. "So you didn't have a meeting with Phillip Constantine tonight?"

"Oh, I met with him. It just wasn't new. The man is so forgetful it took two months to plan the fucking thing."

"Leo," she warns.

"Eva," I warn back. "You came to my house in the middle of the night to scold me for this?"

"I wouldn't dream of scolding you. No one scolds the Beast of Bishop's Landing and gets away with it."

I roll my eyes at her little joke. "You're the only one. Now move on from your scolding."

Eva balances an elbow on the arm of the sofa and pulls a throw blanket over her legs. I lean forward in my chair to take the pressure off my back. My jacket was fucking killing me by the time I got home from my adventure with Phillip Constantine.

And Phillip's daughter.

"I'm not scolding. I just wanted to talk about it."

"It's a long story." I rub both hands over my face. "Long ago, in a city much like this one, there were two families—"

"Leo." Eva's voice has softened and gone wary. I hate when she does this. It's the voice she uses when she's worried about me. No one needs to be worried about me. Not now, and not ever. "Who's this about?"

"The Constantines."

"You know what I mean. Is it me or you?"

"Very bold of you to assume I'd pick on Phillip Constantine just to avenge my favorite sister."

Her dark eyes search mine, and old pain over the ridges of my spine flares to life. "If it's about me, then it's not necessary."

"If it's about you then it absolutely is necessary." Rumors of my uncontrollable temper have largely been exaggerated. Anger is a tool, except when it's not. Right now it's a dog straining at its leash. It growls and snaps its teeth whenever I think about what happened to Eva. No, that's not right—whenever I think about what Lane Constantine did to Eva. "They have to learn, sister mine."

Eva puts her Coke down on the table and folds her hands in her lap. "Lane is dead."

"Everyone in the world knows that."

"He can't learn a lesson from you if he's dead. And he especially can't learn a lesson through his senile brother."

I laugh at that. "Phillip Constantine isn't senile. He's just absent-minded. His signature on my contract will be several times more useful to me because of it. His little invention is going to make me a fortune. How could I turn it down?"

My sister narrows her eyes at me. "If I know you—and I do know you, let's not forget that—then he didn't offer you anything. You made all the offers."

"I'm getting bored with all these hypotheticals."

Eva sighs. "Are you sure it's not about you, too?"

"What, me and my charmed life?"

Her eyes sweep over the way I'm sitting in my chair and she purses her lips. "Yes. You and your charmed life, if that's what you want to call it."

I get up and go to stand by the fireplace. "All that's nothing to me now."

A frown from my sister. "But it's bothering you today. Don't tell me it's not. I can tell when you're lying."

The heat from the fire is pleasant on my arms and legs but a mild and unsexy torture on my back. "I would never lie to you."

She considers this. "You can stretch out on the couch, you know. It doesn't make a difference to me. I can bother you if you're lying down."

"I've been sitting a long time."

"Really, Leo? It's nothing to you? You really never think about it?"

It is a funhouse mirror of bullshit. Pain and confusion all the way down. Do I think of it? No. I never, ever do, except when I'm conscious. Except when I'm aware of anything touching my skin, which is fucking always. "Never."

Eva shakes her head. "Fine. I don't need you to admit it to me. What I do need you to do is leave Phillip Constantine alone. Leave this project of yours alone."

"I'd do anything for you."

She drinks the rest of her Coke, then balances the empty can on her knee. "But?"

"But I'm not leaving Phillip Constantine alone. He signed my contract tonight."

"Forget the contract." For the first time since she walked into this room, it occurs to me that she looks tired underneath her makeup. Exhausted. Winter's short days take it out of her, and everything with Lane didn't make it easier. "Happiness is the best revenge."

"You're not happy."

"I'm happy," she insists, and in her insistence she reveals the full, ugly truth—that she's not happy. That her heart is broken. That she wakes up in the night feeling gut-punched and raw. "I am."

Now I do stride over to the couch and sit down next to her. "Lane broke your heart, and I will be fucked, honestly, if nobody pays for it."

"I knew that was a risk when I got involved with him." A sheen of tears wets Eva's eyes, but she blinks them away before they can fall. "I knew what I was getting into."

"Did you? Or were you too fucking young, and he knew that, and he took advantage anyway? Jesus, Eva, this is about your honor."

"And what about yours?" The fury in her eyes pins me in place, which is an unsettling feeling for a person like me. I'm the one who terrifies people. I'm not afraid of her—never Eva. But we're skirting dangerously close to secrets that might as well be in a locked box in a locked room in a locked house on the other side of the continent. You'd have to be fucking foolish to go there. "What about what they did to you?"

"What about it? You can't expect the Constantines to learn two lessons at once."

"They hurt you." Eva looks like she wants to throw herself across the couch and hug me, which would not be welcome in this moment.

"They hurt you worse," I say.

"Debatable." She looks away from me and into the fire. "We could just forget about all this. Move on with our lives. Never think about the

Constantines again."

Maybe that's possible for Eva. Maybe she can trick her mind into forgetting everything about Lane Constantine and how much he pretended to love her. I don't have that luxury. We were both wounded by the Constantines, Eva and me. But only one of us has a set of inescapable reminders. Even if I never came back to Bishop's Landing again, even if I never set foot in Manhattan, I'd think of those fuckers every single day.

A quiet minute passes. "Is there anything I can say to convince you to give this up?"

"No."

"At least you're honest." Eva hands me her empty Diet Coke can and stands up, stretching her arms over her head. "Am I going to see you at dinner?"

The dinner in question is a Morelli family dinner, hosted like clockwork by our mother. The purpose of these dinners is to let our father pretend he still has any power now that Lucian has taken over Morelli Holdings.

"Yes."

"Promise? It's never any fun without you."

"It's never any fun. But yes. I promise." I won't stop what I've put into motion with Phillip Constantine, but I will sit through dinner, if that's what she wants.

I walk Eva to the front door and see her into the car that's waiting in the drive. Usually, when she looks this tired, she stays over in one of my guest rooms. I let her redecorate two of them last year. It took her three weeks, and she seemed happy the whole time.

She waves to me through the back window. They're tinted, so I can only see the ghost of movement there. I wave back. She pulls away.

The night air is bitter and clear. In a very fucked-up way, it feels better through my clothes than the heat of the fire. After the sound of Eva's car fades, there's nothing but wind through the bare branches of trees in the front courtyard.

A text comes into my phone from one of my people in Bishop's Landing.

She's left home. Heading toward the city.

Haley Constantine isn't going to wait the full twenty-four hours.

It was generous of me, to give her so much time when I wanted to bundle her into the back of my car and bring her here. She was so afraid. That fear would have been fucking delicious in a small space. I would have taken my time undoing the buttons of her coat. Haley, in that ridiculous hat and one mitten, thought I might do it right there against the wall.

I should have.

But something about the trembling bravery in the middle of all that fear made me…

Not soft. Never soft.

Patient. It made me patient. I'm already far more patient than people give me credit for, which is by design. But tonight I outdid myself. Because—fuck. I want to see what's underneath that coat. What's underneath her clothes. My hand should have been at her neck already. It would feel so soft. So vulnerable.

Soon.

I saw the terror in her big, blue eyes. I saw the relief there, too, when she realized that all I'd done to her father was talk him into signing his life's best work over to me. I saw how determined she was to stand in front of him.

No, she won't wait until the sun rises tomorrow. She won't wait, because a night at home in her bed, all safe and warm, would make a girl like Haley lose her nerve.

A gust of wind trails through my sweater and my shirt. My back hurts less now. It's easier to ignore when I'm so fucking excited.

My new Constantine toy will be here shortly. And then we'll play games.

CHAPTER SIX

Haley

MY HEADLIGHTS CUT through the night on a snowy, tree-lined road. It's past midnight. A long drive. The lights from New York City are dim on the horizon in the rearview mirror.

Crystalline snowflakes hover by the dashboard. My breath is a white cloud.

I feel like I've been driving for years. The road rises over a ridge and a gap in the trees opens to reveal a wrought-iron gate set between two stone pillars.

Rick wasn't happy when he saw the neighborhood where I left my car. He insisted on following me to the highway. And then he bailed, because what else was he going to do? Run me off the road and kidnap me?

Not a good look in front of the Constantines.

The gates swing open, and panic surges up and up and up. Leo Morelli is probably stalking the halls of his house, waiting for me to arrive, for the cage to close around me.

My arrival at the end of the long driveway, at the head of a snow-dusted circle drive, cuts off thoughts of cages and traps.

Because Leo lives in a castle.

Towers. Spires. Crenellations lining the roof.

This is not some McMansion in the suburbs. I'm not even *in* the suburbs. This place has *grounds.* It must have cost a fortune, being this close to the city and seeming so far away. When I come to a stop on the drive, my car is facing the most enormous detached garage on the planet, the same antique royal style as the house. It looks like it could have been stables in the distant past. It has four doors, but I bet there are more than four cars inside.

On the front of the castle, stone blocks surround huge front windows warm with light. That kind of light is a trap. It doesn't mean the man inside is warm, or welcoming, or anything but lethal. Two security guards wait at the bottom of a wide staircase leading up to a landing, and the door.

Some of the Constantines talk about the Morellis like they're not powerful, like they're not a threat, but I don't think that's true. I think the men with guns aren't even close to being the most dangerous people in the house.

Two exterior lights make those men and their rifles into silhouettes. My fingernails hurt, and I look down to discover I've been digging them into the steering wheel hard enough to leave marks through my mittens. I tug them both off and toss them onto the front seat.

No delaying the inevitable.

I leave the car running and step out into the snowfall and put a hand to my eyes, temporarily blinded by my own headlights.

God, I wish. I wish it weren't too late to stop my dad from going to that meeting. I wish it weren't too late to explain to him that his family is right about the Morellis, even if they're not right about his inventions. Too late, too late, too late. We're already here.

"Miss Constantine?" one of the men calls.

"That's me." This is a horrible parody of a dinner reservation. They call my name. He's ready for me. My heart beats fast and light, as if it's not powerful enough to actually pump blood. One thought after another crowds into my mind. I could pretend to faint. I could pretend to die. Instead I'll have to pretend to be brave.

"We'll handle your car." One of the men beckons me up the stairs, and they hem me in, one on either side. The guns stay out.

They escort me to a set of oversized double doors set into the front of the porch. I can't tell if they're painted black or if they look black. Either way, the effect is the same. No uninvited guests. I'm expected, at least. They were waiting for me. But now I have to convince Leo Morelli to make a deal with me. I have to convince him to let my dad out of that contract.

It doesn't feel good to be going in with a clutch purse.

They open the door for me and we step inside, into a wide foyer. My heels click on hardwood that shines in the glow of sconces inset in walls with wallpaper—

I'm a Constantine. I still do a double take at Leo Morelli's walls. Dark velvet damask, it looks like, and there's a glint of gold in the patterns. Real gold? I can only imagine how he'd look at me if I asked him. Of course it's real gold. I can hear him saying it. *I'm not a fraud, like the Constantines.*

"This way, Miss Constantine."

And now his security has seen me gawking at the wallpaper. Good.

We take a right and leave the foyer through an archway as wide as the front doors. My heels pinch my feet, but the pain grounds me. I need my wits about me for this meeting. I can't be flying outside my body, paralyzed by the enormity of the risk I'm taking. No. Don't think about that. It makes me lightheaded.

The first man stops at the third door and knocks. His expression remains professionally blank. Maybe I'm imagining the new tension in his shoulders.

"Come in."

I didn't imagine it. His suited shoulders let down a fraction of an inch and he opens the door. "Mr. Morelli, Miss Constantine is here for you."

Leo's unmistakable laugh floats out into the hall and runs a sharp nail down the ridge of my spine. "Don't keep me waiting."

I take the first step toward the door but the other guard stops me with a hand on my elbow. "Your coat, Miss Constantine."

My coat. Yes. My coat. I can't keep it wrapped around me like armor. The point of putting the sexy dress on was to give myself leverage, not hide it beneath a peacoat going soft at the seams. The guard takes my purse while I get out of the coat, and then he holds his hand out for it.

It's hard to let go. But every second that Leo

Morelli waits pounds in my ears. No time to get hung up on a coat. No time to get hung up on going home, and how badly I wish I was there with Cash now. Friday nights are for popcorn and shitty TV, not making deals with the devil. "Thank you," I tell the guard, a beat too late. He motions toward the door, and I go in.

To call this room an office would be funny. Almost flippant. It is an office, with thick carpet on the floor for my heels to sink into and a fireplace heating the air so even a naive woman with a thin, sexy dress on would be warm. This is a magazine office. The ideal office. One wall is taken up with built-in bookshelves. The other is dominated by the fireplace and the two low armchairs in front of it.

The middle is taken up by Leo Morelli's desk.

And Leo Morelli.

The window behind him is rendered black by the firelight, but the man himself looks burnished. Like the fire is his friend. Embers reflect in his dark hair, and shadows play across his clothes. He's not wearing a suit. I expected a suit. Something as expensive as the coat he wore when he hurt those vagrant men for me. But he sits behind his desk in a charcoal sweater, writing something on a sheet of paper in front of him. I didn't know I could feel underdressed in the presence of a man in a sweater, but I do.

He looks up from his paperwork and if I thought his dark eyes were captivating and terrifying in the moonlight—Jesus. That was nothing compared to the glow of the fire. "You're early," he comments.

"I missed you." I pretend my knees aren't quaking and go to sit down at one of the chairs by his desk and run my fingers over the elegant curve of the arms. Another surprise—it's not a hellishly uncomfortable seat. Or at least it wouldn't be, if I didn't have to sit up so straight, and on the very edge. "We were having an interesting conversation."

Amusement lights his eyes, but the laugh he lets out is harsh. "Yes. It's always entertaining to watch Constantines squirm."

My face goes hot. "I love my dad. That's why I'm here."

He gives a dismissive wave of his pen. "No need for theatrics, Haley. Tell me what you're offering so we can get on with this."

"Name your price." My pulse is too big for my body, my breath too shallow. "I'll do what it takes to get him out of that contract."

Leo scoffs. "You'll do what it takes? I don't

think you can, sweetheart. I stand to make a fortune off your father and humiliate the entire Constantine line. That's a win-win situation for me." He tosses the pen down, bored. "And I can have any woman. You're not the worst I've come across, but special? No." His eyes follow the neckline of the dress. "You've got decent tits. A nice size. Big enough to tit fuck, but I've seen better. You have pretty thighs, at least from what I can see in that dress, but nothing to write home about."

I want to burst into a cloud of ash and disappear into the fire. "I'll do anything."

He narrows his eyes and points at his cell phone, perched there on the desk. "There are a hundred women who'd get on their knees and suck my cock if I called them right now. I'm Leo fucking Morelli. Who are you?"

Compared to him? Nothing. I don't have anything to give him except myself. But if I let myself shrink, if I let myself cower, then I lose. I lift my chin. "Is that what you want? For me to suck your cock? For me to get on my knees?"

Forget college. Forget exams. This is the real test, and I'm going to pass it by surviving this moment, this awful, tense moment. Leo Morelli could demand that I get down on my knees on his plush carpet and let him fuck my mouth. He could, and I would do it, and the possibility is worse than the demanding.

Waiting is a knife to soft skin, and he knows it.

That's why he lets that smile slip slowly over his face so I can see his perfect teeth. Leo Morelli knows that he is devastating to look at, so beautiful it hurts, and he also knows that I can't stop looking at him or he will have won everything.

"No, darling. For what you're asking, it's going to cost a lot more than a blowjob. You, in my bed. For a month. That's the deal."

Relief twists itself up with fresh embarrassment. Thirty days of Leo Morelli is a lifetime. An eternity of his voice, confirming my worst fears— that I'm nothing to write home about and never will be. That I'll always be on the outside of my own family. That I'll always be marked by this deal with him, forever and ever, even if I can convince him to keep it a secret.

I don't let the tears show. I don't let my chin quiver. I grit my teeth to keep myself steady and upright. "I'll stay with you a month, and you'll let my father go?"

His cruel eyes test me again, lingering on my

face, on my chest, on my throat. A new terror pulls goose bumps from my skin. He could still decide not to go through with it. Send me out of here with a single word to the men outside. Dismiss me, and hurt my father, and ruin everything.

"God as my witness," he says, the words deliberate. "I'll let him go."

CHAPTER SEVEN

Haley

"THEN WE HAVE a deal." My voice shakes a little, but I pretend it doesn't. I pretend I'm a businesswoman making a business deal and I am not afraid at all of what it means to be in Leo Morelli's bed for a month. "Is there something for me to sign?"

Leo's mouth curves upward in a slash of amusement. "So the Constantine girl wants it in writing."

"Yes. I do. And I want something else, too."

"You're a greedy thing, aren't you? I said I would let your father go. I won't agree to kiss away your tears and tuck you in at night."

The thought of him doing those things is another layer of fire on my face, on my skin. The fact that he expects tears...Jesus. I'm going to be charred at this rate. "I don't want that." It's true enough. I don't want comfort from a Morelli, even if a secret part of me does want to know what it would be like for that mouth and those hands to touch me like that. "I want this to stay between us."

Leo picks up a slim portfolio and moves it in front of him. "Embarrassed to be working with a Morelli, is that it?"

"No." Yes. And embarrassed that the sound of his voice is doing something shameful to me. "My family—we're not like the other Constantines."

"And you're a special girl, not like all the others," he taunts.

"That's not what I mean." I take a deep, steadying breath and keep my hands in my lap, though I want to cover my face so much that my wrists ache. "You know it. You know that we're not in the inner circle. That's why you chose my dad. You knew he would be an easy target."

"He was." Leo laughs. "So desperate to get money for his toys. So trusting…"

My throat aches. Yes, my dad is trusting. Yes, he is naive. Yes, his family let him down, again and again and again. "They'll hurt him if they find out he made a deal with you. Caroline might hurt all of us."

Darkness flickers through his eyes, but it's gone so fast it must have been a trick of the light. "I've already done your daddy a favor, and now you want me to save his sorry ass, too?"

"Yes."

"Christ. I've never met a family more helpless than yours." He opens the folio and scrawls something on the front page, punctuating it with a hard line. "I'm sure you'll find a way to thank me for saving you. Twice, now." Leo flips the folio and pushes it across the table, then holds the pen out. He waits a beat, then shakes it in front of my face. "You could start by not wasting my time."

I take the pen, tears burning at the corners of my eyes. "Can I read the contract before I sign my life away, at least?"

"Your life." Another dark laugh. "Only a month, darling. Are you really so fragile that a month with me would be the end of you?"

Maybe. I ignore him and read the words on the page. I haven't signed a lot of contracts in my life, but it looks pretty standard. It says things like *released from our agreement* and *unrestricted access* and *in exchange for a period of one calendar month or equal to thirty days*. It says *Haley Constantine*. It says *Phillip Constantine*. On one margin, in Leo's clear writing, it says *Agreement between the parties to remain confidential*.

"This is too much." I feel sick with it. Like

I'm hanging off the edge of a cliff by my fingertips. "Unrestricted access?"

"To your body," Leo adds.

"It's too far."

He narrows his eyes. "Is it?" He opens a drawer in his desk and pulls out a sheaf of papers that look horribly familiar. "I, Phillip Constantine, release all claims regarding copyright and trademark to Leo Morelli and Morelli Holdings. The transfer of intellectual property will be complete when a sum of $50,000 is paid by wire transfer." The date for the transaction is today. Yesterday. It's past midnight. The money has already been sent. "I waive all rights to further compensation for the licensing of my intellectual property and indemnify and hold harmless Leo Morelli and Morelli Holdings for any and all personal and professional losses, including those unforeseen."

My face has gone tight. "That doesn't—that's not about one of his inventions."

"You're correct." Leo smiles, the curve vicious in the firelight. "This contract includes all your father's intellectual property. Would you like me to read the clause spelling out what happens to his future inventions?"

I stare at him, disbelieving. Not just the energy project. Not just a decorative invention, like the wind chime. Everything. Leo has taken everything. From now until forever. My father's life's work, gone with the stroke of a pen. He'll never recover. When he realizes what he's done, he'll never recover.

"Or maybe you'd be interested to hear that your father is required to attend all publicity engagements required by me or Morelli Holdings. That would mean press tours, documentaries, interviews…"

Publicity that Caroline Constantine would definitely see. Publicity that she could never allow. She'd kill my father before she let that happen.

I pick up the pen and start with my initials on the line he drew.

The ink is still wet when I put down my mark. It strikes me as almost painfully intimate, that ink meeting. Or it could be that I'm losing it in the face of the next month of my life.

He's done me one kindness, which is that the whole contract is only one page long. I don't have to fumble with the corner of the paper. I sign my name in big, swoopy letters, as if I am not ready to die of shame.

"Good girl." He's sarcastic. Mean. I turn my head to the side like he slapped me. Something in those words makes me want to hear them again. I don't know what. I don't know why. I keep my eyes on the fireplace while Leo signs the document himself. "Gerard."

Leo doesn't so much as raise his voice, but there's movement in the doorway behind me. Another suited man, though his suit is different. More refined than the ones the guards wore. "Sir?"

"Take her upstairs."

"Right now? I thought—" God, I sound so scared. So naïve. "I thought I would be able to get some things from home."

A beat passes, and then Leo laughs, a sound like barbed wire. "No, darling. I've sent someone for that."

Panic. Pure, crushing panic. "But then—"

"Your precious clothes will be here within the hour," he snaps. "Do you have any other requests, or can I move on with my night?"

"No, I don't." I stand up on legs that haven't stopped shaking. Leo's eyes are coals, dark and fiery, and he watches me do it. I should be thankful that I'm not on my knees right now, though that is fully on the table. Unrestricted access is on the table. Those are the terms of the agreement. He's within his rights to take advantage of them at any time. "Thank you."

"Say it again. That was so pretty, coming from a Constantine."

"Thank you."

"For?"

"For—" I'm a ball of tension and nerves and tears and I need to get away from him before he sees me cry. "For saving me from those men. And for making a deal with me."

"You're welcome, darling. Now get out of my sight."

Gerard holds out an arm toward the door and it's all I can do to keep my footsteps measured. "Thank you," I whisper to him when we're out in the hall.

"No need, Miss Constantine." Gerard has the same tense set to his shoulders that the bodyguard did. There's worry in his eyes. He looks like he wants to say more, but then he presses his lips together and shakes his head, the movement almost imperceptible. "This way."

It's late, but a woman meets us back in the foyer. She takes one of my hands in both of hers. "Mrs. Page," she says, wearing a smile that's both soothing and sad. "You must be Haley. Your room is upstairs."

The foyer, with its sconces and gold-stitched

wallpaper, opens onto a grand staircase leading to the second floor. Mrs. Page walks in front of me. Gerard walks a step behind.

At the top of the stairs, the hallway stretches out to either side.

We go left, all the way down to the end, and go past an enormous door set into the wall. "Mr. Morelli's rooms." Mrs. Page gestures at the door, then passes by without stopping. It's obvious now that the house is shaped like a square with a courtyard in the middle. I can see it lit up down below. Windows, everywhere. So much light for such a dark man.

Mrs. Page stops at a door at the opposite end of the hall and opens it. Her smile seems genuine but there's a pinched look around her eyes. She's worried, too. About me? I don't plan to fall to pieces until I'm alone. At home, if I can make it that long. "Thank you," I tell her. It seems wrong not to say it, even though she's ushering me into the place I'll live while I'm Leo Morelli's prisoner. I can't help asking the question, now that we're here. "He said—"

Her expression stays mild while she waits.

"I'm supposed to be with him. In his bed."

Mrs. Page waves this off. "No one sleeps in his bed. At any rate, he owns every bed under this roof. Go on inside."

I should feel more relieved, but a separate room doesn't make him less evil, or me less terrified.

"There are fresh sheets on the bed." Mrs. Page bustles in behind me and picks up a slim remote from the bedside table. Across from the bed, a fire springs to life in its grate. Another button, and a lamp glows from a corner of the room, bathing the space in more warm light.

Warm light for an impossibly beautiful room.

This guest room is positioned on the corner of the house, so most of the walls are windows looking over a landscape sketched in moonlight. I can't see much when it's so dark, but it's not like being hemmed in by a cage. A four-poster bed has been made up, the rose-colored blankets folded open to clean, white sheets. The colors repeat in the pillows and through the rest of the room. My whole body relaxes.

For a second.

A man like Leo Morelli had nothing to do with this room. He couldn't have. It's too inviting. Mrs. Page crosses to the other side and shakes out a blanket that goes on the arm of an armchair by the window. Her eyes meet mine. Oh—she's been waiting for me to finish staring.

"This is beautiful," I manage.

A pleased smile. "Mr. Morelli's sister has a good eye." His sister. Here. Decorating a room? The terrible man in the office and a woman who would make a room like this seem mutually exclusive. "She had the bathroom redone, too."

This is the start of a brief tour. The room turns the corner and a door opens onto a bathroom that's the size of my bedroom and Cash's combined at home. The rose color scheme carries over onto the black floor in dedicated patterns edged in gold. A soaking tub rests beneath another huge window. "This is a guest room?"

"Mr. Morelli has several guest rooms, but only two guest suites." Mrs. Page opens a linen closet to show me where I can find towels. A robe hangs on a hook near the shower. She pats it with one hand. "For you."

I follow her back into the main room, where she picks up the remote from the bedside table. "Lights," she says, pointing to one of the buttons. "Fireplace. Windows."

"Windows? To open them, you mean?"

"If it's too bright, or too dark. Don't have to worry much about privacy. They only look over the grounds." She shrugs. "Comfort, mainly."

I laugh at that, and the sad smile on Mrs. Page's face causes immediate regret. "I'm sure I'll be very comfortable."

It's a lie, but she lets it pass. "And this button is for me. I can bring you any linens you need. I'm not supposed to bring food, but I won't tell if you won't."

Anything except a ticket back home, to my family. Anything except the reassurance that Leo Morelli isn't as bad as he seems. She can't bring that, though half of me wants to beg her to tell me that it'll be all right.

It will be if my family makes it out of this unscathed.

"Thank you for showing me all this." I put on my best, most grateful smile. Mrs. Page might be the only woman I see for the next thirty days and a thousand questions crowd the tip of my tongue. My nerves fire, pulling my lungs tight. She's about to walk out of here, I can tell, and I don't know what happens after that. Maybe Leo comes in and strips away the illusion that this room is safe. "I was going to ask—"

A knock at the door interrupts me, and Gerard comes through, a rolling suitcase dangling from his hand. He swings it into place in the middle of the room. "Your things, Miss Constantine."

"Anything you need." Mrs. Page smiles, and then they're both headed for the door.

Gerard leaves it open behind him, and they're gone. I'm alone with my clutch purse and my suitcase, which seems to have gotten here impossibly fast. What did they say to my brother to get him to pack this? It can't have been my dad. The urge to slam the door closed is so powerful that I can feel the wood under my hands, but I don't do it.

The door won't keep Leo Morelli out. Nothing will. So I leave it open. Let him come.

CHAPTER EIGHT

Leo

HALEY CONSTANTINE IS crying, but she's doing a damn good job of pretending she's not.

From the shadowed hallway I can see inside her room. See her pacing back and forth in front of the door. Her rolling suitcase—a cheap thing, nothing like what another Constantine might own—is open on the floor, and she places her feet carefully to walk by it every time.

She hasn't noticed me yet because she's on the phone. I notice her. I came up here to notice her. The phone call is not what I expected. I expected tears, or sullen staring out the window, or any number of things other than a conversation with her daddy. It's a bit late for that.

"No," she's saying, her expression soft. She's not sniffling or sobbing or doing anything to give away the tears rolling down her cheeks. "I'm safe, Daddy. It's not—no, this is where I should be."

A sigh. She pads back across the carpet. Haley's changed out of the dress she came here in, which is a shame. She's now barefooted in a pair of skinny jeans and a long-sleeved shirt that hugs her body. The shirt is a dusky red color that goes with the room. I wouldn't have thought a Constantine could ever look right in a room that I own, but we've arrived at that impossible moment.

"Dad." Haley puts a hand up over her eyes and keeps walking. The gesture makes my heart ache. It's so sudden and out of place that I put a hand to my chest. The pain is there, a dull hurt, and gone again. So Haley covers her eyes when she doesn't want people to know she's crying. It's information, not a reason to have an emotion or a fucking heart attack.

"Daddy, please. You're making it—" She swallows hard and when she speaks again her voice is level and sweet. "This is the only way. I know. I know. It's the only way out of this, and I promise, it's not so bad. I'm all right. I'll be home soon, and this will all be over."

Hearing her promise it is a knife somewhere in the vicinity of my ribs. That, and something else, too. A feral animal desire. If Haley Constantine thinks that this will ever be over, she's wrong.

Even if I stick to the terms of our contract and let her walk away after thirty days, she'll live with this every second for the rest of her life.

The pain in her voice is what I wanted, anyway. There's no point in playing games with the Constantines if they don't hate it.

"Get some rest," she says. "Yes, you can. You can't spend the next month in your workshop. You have to eat and sleep, and I'm going to tell Cash the same thing. Do not tell Petra. No— Daddy. Don't tell her. The fewer people who know, the better. Did you delete his messages?"

My messages. She's talking about me.

"Good. Now go to bed. It's late, and I'll call you again when I can. Don't worry." The hand comes down from her eyes, a few last tears shining on her skin. "I love you. Bye."

I'm moving as soon as she hangs up the call. Haley senses it, and her eyes go wide. She scrambles to put the phone in the pocket of her jeans and is already backed up against the bed by the time I'm in the guest room. Haley wipes away the tears with her sleeve and stands up straight.

It's too late. I saw her body trying to hide. Good instincts, but I'm going to take them to pieces. I step over the suitcase and get closer, closer, crowding her against the bed. Her lips part, breath coming faster, and it's enough for now to watch her bend and shiver. I lean in. Let her feel the brush of my lips against the side of her neck.

And take her phone out of her pocket.

Her eyes follow it when it disappears into mine. "No—"

"Don't argue." I circle the suitcase, then stand over it. "Don't fuck it up when you're being such a good girl." Haley's cheeks redden at the sharp tone, and she looks down at the floor. "Giving me what I want. Saving your daddy. Fuck, you'd be perfect if you didn't make me help you."

Her blue eyes meet mine. "Help me with what?"

"Unpacking." I kick at the suitcase and some of the clothes inside tumble out. I wasn't particularly kind about the way I demanded the suitcase from her father—and, I'm assuming from the phone call, her brother. I sent my most intimidating foot soldier and gave them ten minutes. It wouldn't be entertaining if they weren't worried sick. "You've left all of this out. You must be having a hard time finding the dresser."

"I can do it. Let me—"

I hold up a hand to stop her, and she folds herself back against the bed. "Oh, no, darling. It's my pleasure. I'll let you watch. How about that? I'll decide what's fitting for you to wear in my house, and you can watch."

Haley stays silent.

The first shirt comes to hand, and it's a twin of the one she's wearing, only in dark green. I hold it up so she can't help but see it. "Cute, don't you think?"

Her tongue darts out to wet her lips. "Yes, but you don't think so."

Oh, I do.

"A Constantine shopping the sale rack." I flip the tag out of the collar. "Target? I'm surprised you didn't get tagged with a dress code violation." I toss it behind me, out the open door. "No. I don't want to see you in that here."

"Because it's from Target?"

"Because it's not sexy."

This is an outright falsehood. The shirt she's wearing shouldn't be sexy in the least. But the way it nips into her waist and shows a bare hint of cleavage is doing frustrating things to my cock.

Another top. I raise my eyebrows at Haley, then toss it out the door. "So you've never seen another Constantine, then."

"I've seen my family." Her chin comes up. "I've been to Constantine parties. If I—" Haley stops herself and tries again. "My brother packed for me."

"Ah. He wanted you to look as unattractive as possible."

"No." This, softer than the rest. "I think he wanted me to be comfortable." She nods toward the leggings in my hands. "Those are my favorite."

I stretch them until the seams pop and the fabric tears. Her eyes follow my hands, my face. The shredded remains of her favorite leggings as they join the rest of her clothes in the pile.

"They're not *my* favorite, darling." Two more tops. Two more pairs of pants. "My god. Your brother is a sadist, isn't he?"

Anger flashes in her eyes, but she gets it under control. "He didn't have a lot of time."

"He had enough to pack this disaster of a wardrobe. Either he genuinely thought these would be appropriate for stepping outside your house or he wanted you to go naked. Twisted." I laugh at the image of that little Constantine boy scrambling to choose clothes for his sister. Thinking he might one-up me, somehow. God help him.

That's the thought that keeps my temper in check. It's hotter by the minute, with every piece of clothing I take from the suitcase. Because, infuriatingly, I like the clothes. The cheap, mass-produced clothes I would never dress Haley in. I wouldn't be caught dead letting her walk around the world in clothes from a discount store.

But I like them on her all the same. The clothes aren't demeaning enough for what I want to do to her—not enough by far. But I fucking like them. Haley is sexy even in those outfits.

It doesn't make sense, which pisses me off. This was supposed to be simple. I planned it that way. Embarrassing Phillip Constantine and using him as bait was going to be easy to execute and easier to profit from, and if I'd known his daughter would show up and be like this, all innocent and embarrassed and trying her level fucking best not to cower…

I still would've done it.

All that's left in the suitcase is a collection of underthings. I hook one of the visible bra straps around my finger and lift it into the air.

Haley watches it, her cheeks a deeper red than I thought possible.

"What's your excuse for this?"

"I didn't want the boys at college staring at my nipples." This, so deadpan and so at odds with the hot red of her face, almost takes me out. Leo

Morelli, dead at thirty-two of a Constantine heart attack.

Just like Haley's shirts, her bra is cute and cheap and flimsy.

There's only one thing for it.

I tear through the lace with my teeth.

She freezes in place, all of her still except the quick rise and fall of her chest. I would give anything to know what she's imagining in this moment, but asking her might give her the impression that I give a fuck.

Maybe I do.

But now's not the time for that kind of intro-spection. It's time for a sleight of hand. A distraction. It's time to embarrass her more. So much that she doesn't notice the state of my cock through my pants. If I can make her cry, all the better.

The bra goes with the other destroyed things, and I reach down into the suitcase for a pair of her panties.

Haley closes her eyes.

"Haley Constantine likes watching her clothes get torn apart by the Beast of Bishop's Landing," I comment. "She likes it so much she can't bear to watch anymore, because she'll ruin her Target panties."

Her eyes fly open again, and her hand goes to her throat, where I want my hand to be. "I'm not turned on by this." A petulant frown, quivering at the edges like she might cry. "I'm not turned on at all."

"Aren't you?"

I let that hang in the air until she looks away.

"You're being horrible."

"I'm being a gentleman." I look her in the eye and pull apart the fabric of her panties, relishing in the way the individual threads snap one by one. "It would be mortifying for you to walk around my house for the next thirty days in these disgraceful clothes."

"You're mean."

"Well, yes, darling. What did you expect out of a Morelli? Some simpering jackass who's over the moon for you?" I pick up the suitcase, walk it to the door, and dump the rest of it out onto the pile. A book tumbles out with the rest of Haley's panties. "Aww. Your brother packed you something to read."

She takes a half-step forward, but I've already abandoned the suitcase and picked up the book. A battered hardcover, the dust jacket missing. Haley hasn't just been reading this—she's read it more than once.

"A fantasy, Haley?" She lets her head fall back, her hair spilling over her shoulders, and I've done it—I've fucking done it. She's more embarrassed about this book than any of her clothes. "A fantasy."

I take the book back into the room and shake it open, balancing the thick spine in one hand. Oh my fuck, I'm delighted. Haley's brother swiped this book straight off her nightstand. I flip through the pages, and Christ, it's perfect. It's so nerdy and sad and fucking adorable.

"Oh, they love each other. This one here says he would wait a thousand years. Does that sort of fuckery get you off?"

"Do all the fake books in your office get you off?"

"How could they? Nothing is as sexy and thrilling as a man with wings." I laugh out loud, and this time no part of it is faked. "A Constantine, escaping into these little fantasies—Christ, darling, you've given me more than you could ever know."

More pages, and Haley tenses. What happens in this fucking book? I skip more pages, scanning for the thing that's making Haley squirm.

Literally. She is squirming, though she doesn't seem to realize it. I have never been so alive as I am right now. I haven't been this aware of another person in years. If I didn't know better, I'd think I was drunk on her impatience and her embarrassment and her red, red cheeks.

My eyes catch on a word midway down one of the pages.

The word is *unleashed*.

Haley is already watching me when I look at her over the top of the book.

I'll do her one better.

"He is unleashed," I read, and she looks toward the ceiling like she's praying for God to strike her down and save her from this. She should know that God does not usually answer prayers. "The dark angel's power burns like fire. It covers me like ash. He's fallen from grace; evil at his very marrow. I should be repulsed, but raw attraction pulls me to him. The steps I take are inevitable. What human wouldn't crave the sensation of those wings wrapping around her body?"

Haley bites her lip. Grips the edge of the bed.

"I let the dark angel draw me close. He wears night and flame like a cloak. He wears his lack of grace like a shield. Without hesitation, he reaches between my legs and pushes two fingers deep inside me. Unerringly, he finds the place that makes me moan. The place that makes me long for sin. He knows how to make me fall, as well."

I fall silent.

Waiting.

Haley doesn't move a muscle.

"The first orgasm wracks me, heightened by his power. I am consumed by him. In thrall to him. Controlled by him. I belong to him, this angel cast out by God. I sacrifice myself to him. It rips the veil from my eyes. Pleasure binds me in its wings and multiplies. He does not allow me to look away. He looks into my soul, and for the first time, I see into his. It's good. The core of him is bathed in angelic light and hope. He is a fallen angel, but he is good. I want to tell him, but I can't speak. I can only moan."

Her face is glowing with fear and anticipation and something else. I was teasing her, mocking her, about being turned on before. I was also correct. I've made it worse.

"This is the kind of thing you think about when you touch yourself at night?" I shake the book in her direction. "This? A fallen angel fucking you?"

She shoots one of her hands out to grab for it.

And misses.

I'm faster, and I have a finger in the pages that

make her blush, so I open the book again and skim to the end of the scene.

The pages are thick and sturdy in my grip. I tear them all out with one hard tug.

I drop the rest of the book on the floor at Haley's feet, then fold the torn-out pages into a neat packet.

She looks hurt by this. As if a few printed pages are more than she can bear. A single tear streaks down her cheek and catches on her jawline, and fuck, I feel that. I feel something. I feel—

"Why?" The word is almost a whisper, laden with exhaustion and pain.

"A promise, darling. I'm going to do all these things to you." I stop at the door on my way out. "*Unleashed.*"

I laugh so she can hear it, and then—yes. A single, choked sob comes from Haley's room.

CHAPTER NINE

Haley

I DON'T PICK up the pile of ruined clothes. I don't bring the suitcase back inside my room. I don't even shut the door.

Once Leo's knife's-edge laughter has faded from the hallway, I fold myself into the bed, pull the covers over myself, and slap the remote on the bedside table until it's blessedly dark.

I do not cry myself to sleep.

What happens is worse. The tears ball up and sit there like a rock, aching and threatening, and I swallow them back again and again until finally I'm too tired to fight them anymore. I expect sobs and I get a deep, heavy sleep. His sister's chosen blankets with a heft to them. They create a calming pressure that keeps me asleep for so long that it's bright when I open my eyes.

White winter light floods the room. I can't believe it didn't wake me up earlier. I fumble with the remote until it's not blinding.

It takes effort to push off the covers and get out of bed. At some point in the night I took my jeans off. I leave them in their puddle by the bed and pad toward the door. Press my ear to the solid wood. Listen.

Doesn't sound like there's anyone in the hall. Then again, I didn't notice Leo coming until he was already in the room. If he's waiting on the other side of the door right now, it'll be simple cause and effect—I'll scream, and then I'll die, and this will be over twenty-nine days early.

He's not waiting on the other side. Neither is my suitcase.

What is waiting on the plush carpeting is a box. It's a pale, pale pink, an echo of all the pink in the bedroom.

I look up and down the hall to make sure no one is watching. A pointless gesture, probably, but I feel alone enough to take the box and close the door of my room. Of the guest room. The room I'm staying in. It doesn't matter.

A satin ribbon keeps the cover on the box, and it falls away with a whisper when I untie the bow. The top of the box lifts away to reveal a layer of white tissue paper in a smooth, perfect line. It feels wrong to crinkle it. But then it also felt wrong to watch Leo Morelli basically bite through one of my bras and shred the lace with his teeth.

His *teeth*.

It made me think—forcibly, because who the hell thinks about Morellis in a sexy way—of how it would feel if I'd been wearing the bra when he did that. If It had been touching my skin. And then I couldn't think at all, because something like that might happen while I'm here. It *will* happen while I'm here.

I shake my head and flip the tissue paper back.

"Oh, god."

It's a prayer to no one, because no one can help me out of this situation. This situation where Leo Morelli or one of his staff has left a box with a lingerie set outside my room.

The message could not be clearer. This is what he expects me to wear.

My skin flushes hot, then freezes. I want to climb back into the bed and stay there for the next twenty-nine days. I'm guessing that's not on the table, so I stalk away from the box on the bed and go into the bathroom.

There's only so long a girl can spend showering and drying her hair and meticulously brushing her teeth. Leo—or his sister, I guess—has stocked the bathroom with everything I could need, and in more expensive versions than I'd ever buy for myself at home. I hate myself more than a little for enjoying the oversized shower with a million settings and the conditioner with the most delicate scent and the hair dryer that's both more powerful and quieter, which should be impossible.

When all of that is finished, when I can't possibly spend another minute applying lip balm, I go back out into the bedroom. The box waits for me there. It taunts me with all the questions I'm forced to confront.

Like—what the hell am I supposed to do now? Put it on, obviously, but then what? Is he going to come approve it, or do I have to seek out Leo Morelli wearing only lingerie?

I take several calming breaths and consider my options. I could call for Mrs. Page with the remote, but that would mean showing her the box and asking her what to do with it. I could put it on and walk downstairs and pretend I'm not embarrassed.

In the end, I go with door number three— wearing my remaining clothes for the second day in a row. The clock on the bedside table says it's almost two in the afternoon.

"Miss Constantine?" There's a brief knock at the door, and then it cracks open. "It's me."

"Hi, Mrs. Page."

"Mr. Morelli is having lunch in the dining room. He'd like for you to join him."

"That sounds great. I'm hungry." I go to the door and throw it open, daring her to comment on the fact that I'm dressed in yesterday's outfit. Mrs. Page's eyes widen for a fraction of a second, and then her face is placid again. "Could you show me where the dining room is?"

The dining room is down on the first floor, roughly underneath the hall with the guest rooms. Mrs. Page takes me to the door and not a step further. "Go on in," she prompts, and then she leaves me standing there.

I go in.

It's a smaller dining room than I was expecting. It has the same elegance as the rest of the house—same high ceilings, same paneled walls—but this is a space built for intimacy. Two dove gray chairs gather near a fireplace on one wall, and a sideboard takes up the other. A silver tray with a matching coffee server and a carafe for cream rest on the sideboard. It's airy in here. Comfortable.

Leo sits on one side of a table made for four people at most, a book open in front of him.

Winter light streams in from the window behind him, throwing all his features into sharp relief. My heart speeds up. He was unbelievably beautiful in the firelight, and the daylight on his cheekbones makes my breath catch.

He looks up from the book and laughs, cruel and short. "Is this how you intend to seduce me?"

"It's how I intended to eat lunch. I'm not sure how anyone could eat in lingerie."

Leo stands up from the table. He's tall. Towering. Dangerous. All things I noticed about him before, but now there are no other distractions. There's only fresh adrenaline and the ringing knowledge that I made a mistake.

I should have worn the lingerie.

I stand my ground while he prowls over to me, circling me like the wolf I know he is. "Do you not understand the terms of our contract?"

"I understand them."

He keeps going as if I haven't spoken. "The terms of our contract include complete access to your body, whenever I want it. And your uniform is at my discretion. I sent you something to wear this morning, and you're here in this." He pinches my shirt between his fingers.

"Mrs. Page said it was lunch." I'm grasping. We both know it. "I didn't think—"

"You didn't *think*." His tone cuts into me, barrels over me. "You're not here to think, darling. You're here to obey. Is it that you'd rather go home and let your father continue on with his contract?"

The words from the contract float back into my mind with terrible clarity.

"No." My lungs contract. I can't get a full breath. "No, that isn't what I want."

"Then you'll have to try a little harder at not being a fucking brat." He's in front of me again, the dark of his eyes lit with gold and flame. Maybe that darkness is anger. Maybe it's not. "You know, I was going to give you lingerie and candles."

"I—"

"But instead, I'll give you what you want. I was going to give you the illusion that it was sex, but now I'm just going to fuck you."

You can't, I want to say. But he can. He will. And I'll have to face the biggest fear of my life, the one I never thought would matter.

Which is that I'm a virgin, and Leo Morelli bought the rights to my virginity.

He has options, in this room. There's his table, and his sitting area, and even the sideboard. He has options, and I don't have any. All the things he could do line up and tumble down in front of my face.

And the worst thing—

The worst part—

The worst part is that I don't hate the idea of them. Being afraid isn't the same as hating. A dark want coils low in my belly. I can't want this, can't even fantasize about it, can't, can't, can't. No part of this is a fantasy, even if my body thinks it is. Even if there's already heat between my legs.

Leo's still watching me. "Strip," he says.

I pull my shirt over my head before I lose my nerve, keeping my eyes on his clothes. He wears another sweater, also black, but it's a different knit than last night. I bite back the urge to make small talk about how often he wears a suit and an overcoat, the way he did last night, on the street. God—it was only last night, and now I'm taking my clothes off for him in his dining room, in broad daylight.

A hand around my jaw brings my attention back to the burn of his eyes. "Focus," he orders. Oh, yes—my hands have stopped moving. Leo drops his hands and steps back to watch me wriggle awkwardly out of my jeans.

I have nothing on underneath.

The last item to go is a T-shirt bra the color of a blue robin's egg. The only one to survive his purge last night, and only because I was wearing it. It falls to the floor next to my jeans and top. They look so sad there. So pathetic. So discarded. I can't take my eyes off them.

"Enough with this shy bullshit. Pick your head up and look at me."

I do it.

It's a shock, every time, because I've always thought evil would make a person ugly. Leo Morelli on his worst day couldn't be described as ugly. He's so handsome it's heartbreaking. My heart shatters with it all over again. So handsome. So cruel.

He crosses his arms over his chest and looks at me, taking an eternity to let his eyes travel over my naked shoulders and my naked breasts and down to my stomach. I want to fold my own arms over my body, but I know he'd be awful about it.

The shivering starts right away. I brace myself for a biting comment, but Leo says nothing. He's too busy watching my nipples pull tight. He watches and watches until finally he steps forward and pinches one between his thumb and finger.

Relief crashes into me—thank god it's happening—and a heightened, desperate fear stomps a heel into that relief. Leo pinches my other nipple and I hear myself make a sound that I've never once made in front of another person.

My gasping attempt to catch my breath makes Leo laugh.

"Oh, who would have guessed?" He pinches that same nipple harder, increasing the pressure until I cry out with it and dig my nails into my thighs, hands shaking. The truth is that I want to grab at his wrist, but I don't want to push him away.

I want to pull him closer.

"Does my dirty girl like this? Does she want more?"

A moan escapes me in response.

Then he *is* closer, but not touching me anymore. Leo's gone back to circling me, this time from inches away. I can feel the heat of his body as he crosses behind me. My knees shake. Anticipation compounds until I could scream, but then his hand comes down on my hip. I angle my elbow to give him room to touch and he rewards it by digging his fingers in, testing the flesh there.

His fingers trail up and up and up until they meet my rib cage and then he goes higher, reaching around from behind me to cup one breast. Too close—too close to my nipples. I arch back on instinct, trying to get away. I'm stopped by his hard body and my mind shuts down. *Don't move. Don't move at all.*

"It's fucking delightful, watching you struggle." He spreads his hand flat on my stomach and slides it down over my belly. I hold my breath. He's getting closer and closer to a place that I want him to touch. Jesus, why? Why? He'd only hurt me. And it might feel good. It's all so very fucked up. "You want to let go, but you can't."

"I won't."

He laughs again. "I'm going to break you, darling. It's only a matter of time. And it's so much fun to watch." The contact lifts, and I suck in a breath that's too hopeful for its own good.

Leo isn't done with me yet.

He's a flash of dark fabric shutting out the world, so close in front of me that I can smell him, smell the clean laundry detergent of his sweater and a hint of expensive cologne and something else, something that must be his skin.

When Leo touches me again, it's to wrap a hand around my throat, using my jaw as an anchor for his fingers and thumb. He forces my head up so I have to look into his eyes.

They're not black like I thought. They're not windows into the black reaches of hell. Or maybe they are, and hell is actually stunning. Maybe hell is the color of deep night and rich wood and, impossibly, gold. Thin striations of gold, just like his wallpaper.

Leo puts his other hand on my shoulder, stroking down my arm like I'm livestock in need of soothing. It works. I hate how it works. I hate how my body goes still and pliant with his hand hovering over my airway. He could choke me, but he's stolen all the tension I'd need to fight it.

He touches my hip and prods at my waist, a mocking smile playing over his lips.

And then.

He cups a hand over my pussy with an even, direct pressure that coaxes my legs apart at the same moment the sensation registers. I let out a strangled gasp. How did he know, how did he know that this would verge on too much, that this would scramble all my nerve endings and turn me into a panting thing hanging from his hand?

This is worse than outright cruelty. Leo's making me look at him, scanning my face—for what, I don't know. But he keeps his hand between my legs, perfectly still.

My ragged breathing is the only sound in the room. I don't know how long he holds me this way, only that I can't think of it directly. It's like looking into the sun.

"That's it." Leo's voice burns the room away. There's nothing left but his hands and his eyes and the perfect bend of his lips. "Prove to me that you're a liar."

"I'm—not. A. Liar."

"Then why are you trying to fuck my hand?" The humiliation is instant and obliterating and I try to get a hand up over my eyes because I'm going to cry. I *am* trying to fuck his hand. Leo gives my face a little shake. "No covering. You can cry, but I'm going to watch."

I try to stop myself, and I can't. Because. I want it so much. I don't know what it is, exactly, I don't know. All I know is that if he stops touching me, I'll die. I try to speak and what comes out is an embarrassed moan.

Leo strokes one finger over my wet slit.

If it weren't for his hand on my jaw, I'd be on the floor. My knees are nothing. My legs are nothing. The only thing they're good for is spreading open for him, which I cannot stop myself from doing.

"Hmm." His tone is bored, but his expression is so intense that I can't breathe. "That was fine, but…" This time, two thick fingers, and he changes the angle of his hand so it's pressing against my clit. My hips work into a frenzy. I wasn't going to come, wasn't going to let the idea cross my mind, but now I need it to survive. Leo pulls his hand away and slaps me hard between my legs. My shocked cry doesn't stop him from working his hand back over my pussy. "You're not going to come today unless it's on my fingers."

Those fingers are already circling my opening. "What if I can't?" It's honesty I didn't want to give him. Didn't mean to give him.

A delighted laugh. "Was your pretty Constantine cunt too tight to take your boyfriends' fingers?" He pushes two of them inside, up to the knuckle, and the breath goes out of me. It *is* tight. Leo's expression shifts, and he works them in a little farther. I am hopelessly, shamefully desperate for him to put them all the way in. It's going to hurt. I want to know that hurt. "Christ. No one has ever finger-fucked you?"

"No one has ever done that."

"Done what?" he asks in a taunting voice. "Say the words."

"No one has ever f-f-fucked me. In any way."

The sound he makes is more of a growl than anything else, and I hardly have time to hear it before he's driving his fingers in deep. As deep as they'll go. He's holding my head up, or it would be dropped back. I see stars. God, it hurts. His fingers are too big but the stretch feels good in a way that makes me so ashamed that I *do* cry.

Leo swipes a thumb over my cheek and it comes away wet. He leans in, murmuring something into my ear, and I don't know what it is because I'm both the size of the universe and shrunk down to the sensation of his fingers invading me. I swing wildly between the two until I come back to my body and find myself in Leo Morelli's dining room, his fingers inside me and one thumb circling my clit.

It's too much sensation to be embarrassed about. I tighten on his fingers in the same rhythm he's using on my clit. It's a relentless rhythm. Soft, like he knows that any harsh movements will push me over the edge into something dark and terrible. Insistent, like he knows that he can't stop. He can't leave me like this. Pleasure builds from his touch, it's hot, hot, hot and getting hotter. Multiplying. Something pulls tight between my legs and I let my weight fall onto his hands, all of it. I can't hold myself up because that coil winds down and explodes.

I come all over Leo's fingers, just like he said I would. I can't enjoy this. I can't like this. I cannot like what he does to me.

It's only when I'm coming down that the words he's saying regain their meaning. *I'm going to break you, darling. It's only a matter of time.*

The aftershocks come one after the other, and slowly I become aware of the pieces of him again. His eyes. His mouth. His sweater. As soon as my feet are back on earth he pulls his hand from between my legs and wipes it across my bare chest. Tears drip down after it, and for an instant I see pain and lust in his face.

Gone in a blink.

He goes back to the table and takes his seat, flipping the page in his book like I was never here. "Mrs. Page will bring a tray up to your room." Oh my god. He's sending me away. "Do better tomorrow."

CHAPTER TEN

Haley

I DON'T SEE anyone on the way back to my room, but they see me. I'm sure of it. This is a huge house, and Mrs. Page and Gerard can't be the only people here aside from Leo. They can't be the only pairs of eyes. The saving grace is that I'm crying too hard to notice.

This is sick and wrong, what he's doing. But more than that, how I feel is sick and wrong. My family would be ashamed of me. Caroline would eject me from the family if she knew that I'd let Leo Morelli touch me. And if she knew that I liked it?

I slam the door to the guest room behind me and sprint for the bed. Someone came to make it while I was gone and I shove the covers back with both hands, ruining their hard work. I don't care. I don't care. I pull all those heavy blankets over my head and sob into the pillow.

If Caroline knew how confused and turned on

I was right now, she'd do worse than excommunicate me. She'd send Ronan after me, and she wouldn't stop there. Cash and Petra would be implicated too, and my dad. We'd all be in danger of Caroline's henchman.

Why is he like this? The blankets are so heavy they make it hard to breathe, what with the crying, so I turn them back and pull them tight over my shoulders. I've never met someone as cruel as Leo and I can't understand what made him this way. I've always known the Morellis were bad people, evil people. Every Constantine knows that. It was abstract knowledge before. Almost academic.

Leo is not mean to me in a generic sense. It's personal. He sees all my weak spots and pushes on them until they bruise. These are not the casual insults of a bully. They're the calculating cuts of someone who knows pain like he knows the back of his hand. Like he knows what it feels like when a Constantine comes on his fingers against her will.

I put the pillow over my face and cry harder. It wasn't against my will. I wanted it. Was desperate for it. And now I'm desperate for more.

For more contact. For more answers. Who hurt Leo Morelli? Who turned him into a beast?

I drop into a hungry, exhausted sleep before I can come up with an answer. The rest of the day turns around this nap. Every time I open my eyes the light is dimmer. A dream pins me to the bed like the blankets. A room full of roses and white. A dark-haired man. He looks like Leo and then he doesn't. His face is softer and more open and in the dream it makes me cry.

A sound pulls me up from a parallel dream about Leo's hands and the dining room. Part by part, my body comes back into existence under the covers. Sheets rest gently on my shins. I've pushed the blankets down to my waist. Still naked. Still here.

The sound, it turns out, was a tray. A stand has appeared from somewhere and the tray balances there with a covered plate and a steaming mug.

It's morning.

I throw my legs over the bed and stand up. Sleeping for a small eternity made my knees less wobbly, but my abs are sore like I've been doing crunches, or trying to ride a man's hand in my dreams. Shake that thought away. Not this morning. I lift the silver cover on the tray.

The plate underneath is beautiful, with a thin gold line around the edges. Leo Morelli owns fine china. I would never have guessed. And the food on top—

Scrambled eggs like small clouds. Three strips of crispy bacon.

And.

And.

A stack of tiny waffles. Silver-dollar sized. My face goes into a cute emoji expression and I can't stop it. Won't stop it. There's a little dish of syrup on the tray, too.

Secondhand embarrassment heats my cheeks. Someone must have felt bad for me. Not Leo, so…another person who saw me trailing up here in tears. The feeling is gone by the time I tuck myself back into bed with the tray balanced on my lap. Hunger comes first. Embarrassment later. These weird, conflicted feelings I have about Leo can go away forever.

I eat every bite of the food. It's the perfect amount, gone when I can't take another bite, and I put the tray back on the stand and stretch. There are no clothes left, but there is the nicest shower I've ever stepped foot in.

There's a box on the bed when I come back out. My heart thumps at the sight. A gorgeous, pale pink box. A black ribbon. There's no pretending I don't know what this is, no excuse to be made. Whatever is in that box, I have to wear.

I wrap the robe tight around my waist and stalk over to the box. Rip away the ribbon. Throw off the top. My heart won't settle. The hairs on the back of my neck pull up. It'll be worse than yesterday. It will be more demeaning, more humiliating, and I know there's no chance he'll let me stay in this room. The tissue paper tears in my hands.

It's clothes.

Real clothes, not lingerie.

That's not completely right. It's real clothes *with* lingerie. The set is the same color as the box, but the dress isn't—it's deeper, like the shirt he took from me yesterday. Of course, it's no Target dress. It's sweet and soft, with sleeves that go down to my wrists. It's long enough to skim above my knees. I twirl in it in front of the mirror and push it back into place as soon as I can. Embarrassing. Embarrassing, to feel nice like this, in a place like this, with a man like this. He's dressed me up like an innocent little doll.

There are shoes to go with the dress. Soft ones, for inside the house. With all of it on I look, shockingly, like a Constantine. Like someone who's never wanted for money or worried about student loans or driven home with snow pouring in through her car's vents.

It's afternoon by the time I get up the courage to leave.

No one has knocked on the door all day. They've left me to dry my hair and lie on the bed and stare at the ceiling. The appeal didn't last very long, so I creep out into the silent hallway.

No sign of Leo, or Mrs. Page, or Gerard. No sign of anyone. Maybe I was wrong about there being more staff than I thought. I pad down the hall and down the stairs to the first floor.

Right or left?

I go toward the dining room. This wing of the ground floor seems to be the less public one, though I'd have to go snooping in order to confirm it. All I really know is that there's a dining room this way.

The door to the dining room is open. It's empty.

So are the other rooms. A formal sitting room. What looks like a miniature art gallery. I turn the corner. I'm underneath the bedroom wing now. Unlike upstairs, where the hall is all windows on one side and doors on the other, this space is all doors.

Someone is humming.

I follow the sound past two more closed doors

to an open one.

Inside the threshold is a den. Brighter than the main hallways, with all that charcoal and gold. The space is all warm wood and leather furniture. It's huge, for a den, or maybe I'm only comparing it to the den in my house, which is basically a cramped closet next to my dad's workshop. The courtyard windows make everything gleam with winter light.

Especially the woman on the sofa, who is lying with her back in the center and her legs flung over the arm. Dark curls spill onto the leather, and her hands—one holding a sketchbook, the other holding a pencil—sparkle with rings. The size and shape of the jewels say *diamonds*.

I take the first step through the door and she twists on the sofa, pushing herself up to look at me. It's sexy. I don't know how a person could make their hair fall that way in a scramble on the sofa, but she does it. "Oh, good." A wide smile lights up her face. I know that face. It's a Morelli face. She looks just like Leo. "You're awake."

"Hi." I run my fingers through my hair, then put my hands back at my sides. "I'm Haley."

"I know." She gets up off the couch and comes to me, barefooted and graceful and…bubbly. Her sketchbook is abandoned, but she doesn't seem to mind. She throws her arms around me. I stand there, rigid, like I've never been hugged before. What's hugging protocol among the Morellis? God. Of all the things to think about.

"Um…" I sound like a shrinking violet. She squeezes, then lets go. "I don't know who you are. I'm sorry. I'm new here."

"Daphne Morelli, pleased to meet you." Daphne's laugh matches her smile—it's personable and pretty. I'm through the looking glass. In some universe where it's possible for a Morelli to be nice to me. My heart shrinks back. She's probably faking it. Probably skilled at making people believe she's kind. But she doesn't seem duplicitous. "Come sit, come sit. I don't have to be anywhere for a while."

I follow her back to the couch. "Weekend plans?"

"I'm meeting a gallery owner about some pieces." Daphne takes a seat on one end of the sofa, then pats the spot next to her. She waits until I'm seated, then pulls a throw blanket off the back of the sofa and tosses it over my lap. "There. Now, tell me why you're here. Leo wouldn't."

What *did* he tell her? Not my last name. If she

knew that, she wouldn't be this welcoming. Would she?

I fold the edge of the blanket over and smooth it out. "It's complicated."

She rolls her eyes. "That's what Leo would say. And then he would laugh." She impersonates his laugh, and it's so close that I laugh too. Daphne's version has none of the barbs that Leo's real laugh does. "Are you in college?"

"English lit." I'll have to go back for the spring semester, when this is all over. Go back to college and pretend I'm the same as I was. "I graduate in the spring."

"Oh, fun. I just graduated. Do you know what you want to do after, or are you still deciding?"

"I'm just trying to survive until graduation." Admitting it feels good. Watching her break into a smile and laugh again, a kind laugh, feels better. It also feels bizarre. Morellis aren't supposed to be like this. They're supposed to be cunning and cruel and ambitious. All of them. "Then we'll see. Maybe I should move somewhere warm."

This, unlike the books I've been reading, is a real fantasy. I'm not going to move anywhere once I graduate. Cash doesn't deserve to look out for our dad by himself while he gets ready for college. When my thirty days are up, I'll be going back home for spring semester and I'll stay home.

I swallow against pain. "What about you? What kind of art are you going to look at?"

Daphne leans in, eyes bright. "I'm not looking, I'm selling." She picks up her sketchbook from the couch next to her and hands it to me. The page is full of curls and swoops that suggest water and movement. It's gorgeous, and she's only used two colors—blue and black. "I'm obsessed with the ocean lately. I've figured out a way to make the waves look alive. I want to do my room like that. A whole wall of nothing but the ocean. For now, I want to put up some of my smaller pieces for sale." She straightens up again with a rueful sigh. "I hope the guy at the gallery isn't freaked out by Leo's security team."

I raise my eyebrows at Daphne, and she groans good-naturedly. "Leo thinks the dealer is shady, so he made me come here first. Apparently my own bodyguard isn't enough for the situation. I reminded him that I'm an adult woman and I can take care of myself, but you know how he is."

"Intense," I supply, because that's the kindest way I can think to describe him.

"Yeah," Daphne agrees. "Protective. Maybe to a fault." A memory curves up the corners of her lips. "One time, this jackass was mean to me in middle school. It was the first week of sixth grade, and I came home crying, and Leo saw." Her eyes go distant, and she shakes her head a little. "Leo waited for him the next day after school. Scared the shit out of that kid. I made him promise not to beat him up, but maybe it would have been better if he had. He can be prickly when he's mad. Whatever he said haunted that guy for life."

Prickly—more like serrated.

Daphne shakes herself out of the memory and picks up her sketchbook, tucking it close to her body. "Anyway, everyone was so nice to me after that. I probably had the best middle school experience in history."

I can imagine it. I couldn't have yesterday, with Leo's fingers inside me and his voice in my ear. But I believe Daphne. It's unsettling to think of him with this hidden side. It's easier to hate a cartoon villain. And if he's not a cartoon villain, what is he?

The conversation turns back to paintings of the ocean. Daphne's in the middle of telling me about her art when she trails off, her eyes sliding to a point behind me. Another big smile. "You didn't tell me she was fun, Leo."

I turn around to see him standing just inside

the threshold, expression lightly scolding. It reminds me of the way he looked in my dream. "You were supposed to meet Gerard fifteen minutes ago, not snoop around in my den. I should have you thrown out for trespassing."

His sister sticks her tongue out at him. "You wouldn't and you know it," she sings, and then she's by his side, rising up on tiptoe to kiss his cheek. I focus all my energy on keeping my own mouth shut, keeping my own jaw off the floor. That anyone, *anyone*, would be this way with Leo is as much a shock as the rest of him. She moves to put her arms around his waist, but he deflects her, turning the gesture into a fast hug he's in control of. The way he does this is so natural, over so quickly, that I wonder if I made it up.

Leo pushes her gently toward the door. "Go to your gallery. I have plans."

"Be nice," she admonishes him, and goose bumps rise on my skin. Apparently he's capable of being nice, if his sister is to be believed, but trusting a Morelli seems like a mistake. Then she's gone, leaving us in the quiet of the den with the crackling fire as the backdrop.

I stand up and smooth down my dress. Put the blanket back in its place. Brace myself to hear how terrible my dress looks, or how he can't believe a person with as little sense as me even managed to put it on the right way.

"Have dinner with me," he says.

I blink, startled. "It's early for dinner. Isn't it?"

Leo looks out the window, seeming almost human. "It'll be dark in an hour. Be in the dining room then."

CHAPTER ELEVEN

Leo

HALEY APPEARS AT the door to my dining room five minutes early, wearing the same wine-colored dress I sent up earlier. The high color in her cheeks tells me she put on the lingerie, too.

Good. She's learning.

She's also coming to grips with the fact that her father failed her. The dress she's wearing cost more than any bargain-hunter could dream of spending. It was made for her last night. Let her think of me every time she puts on a rough, shitty T-shirt from some rack under cheap fluorescent lights.

Haley's eyes go from me to Gerard, who's here to tell Mrs. Page when it's time. "Can I come in, or did you want to finish your chapter?"

I flip my book closed and hand it to Gerard. He takes it without comment. It's a copy of the book Haley had in her suitcase, but this one has its dust jacket stripped off and has been rebound into smaller sections. No one is going to see me reading that trash. Then, because she's still standing in the doorway like a little Constantine fool, I go to collect her. "This is how you enter a room for dinner. Not by planting yourself in everyone's way."

I hold a hand out to her and she takes it. Lets me guide her into the room, which I've had dressed in soft lights and candles. I pull out her chair for her and her face gets redder at the sarcastic politeness.

"Thank you." Her lips barely part to let the word out.

"Mm. It's hotter every time you say that." I make it sound like a lie, but it's not. Every time Haley thanks me it makes my imagination run wild. Through tears, it's even better. With my cum on her face? Plenty of time to find out.

Haley's eyes go to my hands on the back of the chair and she bites at her lip. Once she's seated, I take my place. "How did you like your conversation with Daphne?"

Haley studies my face, no doubt wondering if this is a trap. It's not. I'm going to have a fucking conversation with her. I was irritated that it didn't happen last night. I have no explanation for this irritation. "She's lovely," she admits after several beats. "She told me about going to an art gallery."

The door at the side of the dining room opens, and Mrs. Page steps out, plates and wine balanced on her tray. "And what did you tell her?"

"Mostly about school." Halcy leans back to give Mrs. Page room to pour her wine. Her eyes follow the food on the plate. When my wine is poured and my plate is set, she leans in and eats a prawn. "Thank you," she murmurs to Mrs. Page, who leaves with appropriate speed. Then, to me: "I'm going to graduate next semester."

Her eyes come back to mine at *semester* and a certain delight sparks down the middle of me. A challenge. From Haley Constantine. Two minutes into dinner. She's daring me to break our contract and live up to the evil Morelli name. "And you'll have a degree in…"

"English literature."

"That explains the garbage you've been reading."

"Be honest." Her fork hovers over her plate. "You liked it, too."

I smile at her and watch her pupils expand, her breath catch. "It made me laugh. It was so tame. Just right for a sweet Constantine girl to get off on."

Haley flushes, glancing down at her plate, but recovers. Her chin comes back up. "It could be worse."

"How so?"

"I could be like you. Nothing is good enough to get you off."

If only she knew. If only she fucking knew. It takes every ounce of effort not to crush my fork in my fist. The hours I spent last night, after I sent her up to her room—Jesus. I want to fuck her until she cries. Tears are beautiful on a face like hers. Never mind how this is all supposed to be a game. A rigged game. A game that only I can win.

She's trying so hard to keep herself in check that her trembling energy fills the space between us and tumbles out. I could make her cry now. It would take a few comments at most.

But if I want to hurt her, to make her pay a real price for her family, then I have to draw it out.

I go to speak and find that my teeth are gritted against something nameless and powerful. "When you graduate…" I hunt for a question. A dinner-appropriate question. "You'll have done some internships."

Haley's shoulders relax. "Two, actually. There are a bunch of different publishing companies in

the city. I should have done more, but..." She
trails off. Takes a bite of her food.

"But?"

"Money is tight. Time is short. I try to be
around for my dad and Cash." Her big, blue eyes
come back to mine. "What about you? You seem
close with your sister." A deep breath. "How
many siblings do you have?"

Bizarre. "You already know that."

"Not all of it. The Morelli family tree isn't
considered polite conversation at the Constantine
parties. The ones I've been to, anyway."

I dismiss my first, second, and third responses.
"I have four sisters and three brothers. And you
have two siblings. Your father can't stop telling
people about you."

She swallows hard. "What about your dad?" A
beat. "Do you see him often?"

"Not often. At family dinners, mainly." After
Lucian took over for him, he retreated into the
Morelli family mansion, where he pretends he's at
the center of everything. I see him at my mother's
dinners, which he spends glowering at the head of
the table and barking pointed questions at anyone
in reach. I see him most often in my nightmares,
with a belt in his hand. I'd rather die than admit
that. "Did you learn anything from your intern-

ships?"

"Of course, Mr. Morelli, and I can also tell you my greatest strength and weakness."

It catches me off guard, both the thought of a Constantine having to sit for an interview and Haley choosing this moment to joke about it, and the laugh it pulls out of me is a genuine one. A proud smile streaks across Haley's face and she celebrates this tiny victory with a sip of her wine. "Why did you choose English lit?"

Her grin softens. "My mom taught me how to read. We spent a ton of time together with our books before she died. Sometimes I can still hear her voice when I'm reading." Haley risks a tentative glance from under her eyelashes, then puts her wineglass down with studied care. "Is your mom a reader?"

I hate the cold, defensive feeling I get when the words land. A cousin to jealousy. The only reason I let this continue is because I like the sound of Haley's voice, and I like it more than I thought I would. "She spends most of her time planning dinners and keeping secrets from my father." Fuck—too far. "I'd imagine she reads magazines."

Haley doesn't dare ask what secrets I mean. There are more than we have time for, even if I did want the Constantines to know about how my mother's true fixation is on sleeping with younger men. More than a few of my friends from high school and college went to her bed, right under my father's nose. It was a life-or-death gamble. I have no idea how she's still alive.

The moment is saved by Mrs. Page coming back to serve the main course, which is sea bass. Haley waits until she's gone to speak. "Daphne said you were protective of her growing up."

"And?"

"Did you really make her take extra security to the art gallery?"

"Does Daphne strike you as a liar?"

"No." She cuts into the fish. "But you don't strike me as that kind of person. You know…" A bite of sea bass. Her hand shakes around her fork. "A nice person. A person who goes out of his way for anyone."

"I went out of my way for you."

"To be nice?" Her voice is deceptively casual, as if we're having a conversation about the weather. Her eyes are a sharp, brilliant blue. She thinks she's unpacking me. I hope to hell she's not.

"I was in the right place at the right time." Of course, I was in the right place for Haley because I put myself there. I did the same thing for my siblings.

All except Lucian, who never seemed to feel fear or pain or anything else.

Our parents, on the other hand, hunted for fear and pain. Thrived on fear and pain. Live long enough with a pair of snarling wolves, and it's obvious that the only distraction is a snarling wolf who's foaming at the mouth and snapping at their heels. I was angrier than they were, and crazier, and more reckless as long as it gave my siblings time to hide.

My reputation as the Beast of Bishop's Landing is accurate, it just lacks context.

Old tension strings itself through my muscles. The instinct to blame Haley for it is stronger than the whispers that say it's not her. It can't possibly be her. It's that dinners were dangerous, volatile things, when all of us were forced to be in the same room and there weren't enough exits. When any question from my mother or father could turn out to be a grenade with the pin already pulled.

"Enough about me, darling. I want to know why your family has hung you out to dry in this job market. The famous, perfect Constantines couldn't scrape up a publishing company for you to work at?"

Haley looks uncomfortable. "I never wanted to ask for help. My dad was never a model Constantine, and with my aunt, there are always strings attached."

"Your aunt?"

"Caroline."

Before Haley's mouth is finished forming the word, before the sound can fully reach me, a blaze of anger overtakes its boundaries and burns itself through every one of my veins. The rage takes me by surprise. I was ready for this. I knew the name she was going to say.

Because I know all about Caroline Constantine.

I know all about her from personal fucking experience.

The skin on my back crawls. Phantom pain. Very real fury. It's not about the young woman sitting across the table. Not her fault, anyway. But she's the one who will feel my wrath. Because the world isn't fucking fair. I learned that young. Younger than Haley is now.

I've been holding back. I haven't fucked Haley yet, because I wanted her to spend as much time as possible in horrified anticipation, fearing it, wondering when it would happen. I wanted the monster in her head to be far more terrifying than reality, so the two of them—me and that frightened imagination—will feed off each other until she cries and begs and comes and lives the rest of her life with the mark of them on her heart.

It's disappointing, in a vague sense, that I only managed to wait two nights. But I'm ready now. Ready for a revenge fuck. Ready for *the* revenge fuck. Haley can be the one to answer for all the crimes of the Constantines. Then she'll know—

She's gone on speaking. Awareness of it comes too late to understand what she's saying. I discover I'm staring at Haley, into those blue Constantine eyes, and not bothering to make my expression into something that passes for neutral.

Too late. Haley's already seen. She hooks a hand on the edge of the table, holding on so tight her knuckles are white.

"Leo?" The tremble in her voice says she doesn't recognize me.

Or maybe it says she does.

CHAPTER TWELVE

Haley

I'VE SAID THE wrong thing.

Leo's face is a candlelit mask, the shadows deadly sharp. It's subtle. I expected his fury to be a massive display, with bared teeth and extended claws. With flipped furniture and broken glass. But whatever wound I've opened with my words is contained within his body.

It's worse that way. Scarier. A man who turns over tables—I can understand that. I can fathom an anger so overwhelming that it transforms to blind motion. I've felt that before. When my mother died I tore down the curtains in our house. I ripped at the seams to her pillow until the soft insides bled out on the bedroom floor. For months afterward, we could only use paper plates and cups.

He's that angry. The air is hot with it. But Leo does nothing. The flames from the candles burn in the black centers of his eyes. He sits up tall, his fork held so carefully in one hand that I'm afraid for it.

Or maybe I'm afraid for me.

At the sound of his name, Leo's jaw tightens.

The door behind me—the one Mrs. Page keeps coming out of—opens, and the pattern of her steps falters. She feels it, too. I'm aware of a shadow in the other door. Gerard. He's been in and out, holding the door for Mrs. Page and carrying things for her.

I try to catch her eye when she puts the dessert plates down in front of us.

She won't look at me.

"Close the door when you go out." Leo's voice is deadly even.

Mrs. Page pauses, halfway to standing, then completes the movement. "Can I bring more water? More wine?"

"No. Leave." Leo keeps his eyes on me. Mrs. Page takes our empty plates. Leo drops his fork at the last second and she takes that, too.

My heart beats fast, heels lifted off the floor, ready to run. Gerard closes the door to the hall. Mrs. Page is gone in a heartbeat, the kitchen door swinging behind her.

"Get up."

"What did I say?" Releasing my grip on the

table seems like a bad idea. But then, so does staying in my seat. I push my chair back and stand up. "Tell me what I said."

Leo blinks, and his face is transformed. He's angry, yes—I can see it in the skin around his eyes. But taunting, now. Skin-deep. He uses this anger. He doesn't just feel it. "It doesn't matter, darling. What matters is that you signed a contract."

The backs of my arms pull tight with goose bumps. "I thought we were having dinner."

"There are no exceptions for meals." He laughs. "Did you think you would be excused from your obligations as long as you had food in your mouth? Come here."

He pushes his own chair back, creating space between his body and the table. It's obvious where I'm meant to go. Two days ago I might have hesitated. Now my feet start moving before the fear can settle down.

It feels too close to the table, and too close to him. He's tall even when he's sitting down, and I don't know what to do with my hands next to this cruel, beautiful devil.

"Take your clothes off." I reach for the dress. Pull it over my head. The lingerie he bought me is a perfect, delicate fit, and I feel the smallest drafts from the air on my skin. On my nipples. Leo tests one with his thumb and I shiver. "You look better in something other than rags. Do you think," he muses, "that I meant for you to leave anything on?"

"I thought you might want to take the lingerie off yourself." Lie, lie, lie. I didn't think. I just obeyed him, because that's what I agreed to do. Because I'm too afraid not to. Because I don't want to admit that part of me is afraid that I want to do what he says. That I get some kind of sick pleasure out of it.

A dangerous grin. "What a good girl. You thought so hard, and you were almost right." Why? Why does it hurt to hear him be so mean, so mocking, and why do I want him to do it again? "If I have to take it off, then it won't survive the taking. Do it yourself, and do it now."

There's not enough room for the way my body has to twist and turn to get out of my shoes and panties and bra. Leo doesn't make it any easier. He lets me brush against his legs, lose my balance, catch myself in time to keep from touching him. Stand up, with a hot face and a racing heart. Let it happen already. Let it happen.

He stands up too, towering over me. Leo strokes three fingers down the side of my neck and then his hand is there, firm, on the boundary between holding and choking.

It happens again. My body goes still, all the tension concentrated under his palm. Leo looks down into my eyes. It's a searching look. I don't know what he hopes to find. He's close enough to kiss me. The inches between us stretched tight. If he kissed me this way—if he did—

Leo looks away, and the loss of his eyes on mine causes a tumbling sensation. He keeps his hand where it is while he reaches around behind me. In the process my naked breasts brush against his shirt, one nipple catching on a button, and I gasp. "So impatient." The comment is almost to himself. "The Constantines don't teach women how to wait for anything, do they?"

A plate clatters against the linen tablecloth and his shirt is rough against my skin. It's softer than I would expect a man's shirt to be but it might as well be sandpaper. It's too much. It's not enough.

Something snaps behind me, and Leo brings whatever it was in front of my face. Chocolate. A piece of chocolate. It was decorating the dessert. He squeezes at the bones of my jaw and I open my mouth. I have to open it. He's making me.

With fierce concentration, with that same

pointed anger, he puts the chocolate on my tongue.

"Close."

I clamp my teeth shut. The chocolate starts to melt right away, and my god, it's good. It's rich person chocolate. It's the kind of chocolate only a Constantine with real money would have.

Or a Morelli.

He backs me up a step so my ass hits the table. "Lie down on the table, unless you want to test your theory. Don't swallow."

I was about to, but I don't. I push myself up onto the table with sweetness on my tongue. Chilled sweetness. I wonder if the chef knew they were doing me a favor. It's awkward, lying down on a dinner table, but I ease myself back.

Leo sits down, and then his hands are on my thighs. I have enough leverage to get my head up, to look at him. He looks me in the eye while he spreads my legs.

Wide.

And then wider.

I'd be panting, afraid and turned on, if I didn't have to keep the chocolate in my mouth. He watches my face until it's unbearable.

Then.

His eyes go between my legs. I try to close

them but his hands keep them apart. He doesn't comment on this. Doesn't touch me. He's had his fingers there, but he waits. I never knew patience could be so mean.

"It's getting harder now, isn't it? It's starting to melt and get fucking everywhere. All you can taste." One thumb traces a slow path on the inside of my thigh. "It didn't seem like much in the beginning, but now you could choke on it."

I find myself nodding. Find the beginnings of tears in my eyes. From frustration, overwhelm, I don't know.

"Awful." He sounds pitying, and that's the worst, because I know it's not real. Can't be real, coming from him. "Touch yourself. Like you do when you're all alone at home."

I shake my head. "Can't," I say around the chocolate. "I can't. Too embarrassing."

Leo leans back in his chair, giving himself more room to look between my thighs, but keeps holding them apart. "You're too embarrassed, but you're wet. I can see it from here. This is turning you on. Here's your choice, darling. You can put your fingers on that pretty clit like a good girl, or I'll do it for you. And if I have to do that—"

I put my hand between my legs, fingers skimming my clit. Dying. I'm dying. But it feels good to be touched, even if I'm the one doing it. God. It doesn't get worse than this.

"You don't keep your hand still when you're in your bed." He slaps the inside of one thigh. It stings. The sting of his tone hurts more. Both of them together send my fingers into motion. This isn't how I do it at home, but I can't remember exactly what I used to do, and all that matters is not disappointing him. I do not want to disappoint him. It is so fucked up.

And it's working. Pleasure starts a slow build between my legs, all caught up in the humiliation and the heat across my cheeks. Oh, god. Oh, no. It's going to be terrible and so, so good.

"Swallow," Leo orders, and I do, without thinking.

"Thank you," I tell him, also without thinking.

He laughs, low and mean. "Tell me about your boyfriends."

I wish for the chocolate.

Another slap to my thigh, hard enough that I cry out. "Tell me about all the things your boyfriends did to you while they weren't fucking you, and keep your fingers moving."

I let my head drop back because it's too hard to keep everything coordinated and suffer through this horrible, hot moment. "My first boyfriend only kissed me. He wasn't good at it." I sound lightheaded, and it's because I am, because I can't get a full breath. "The next one touched me."

"Where?"

"Over my bra." Leo slides one hand up and takes my breast in his hand, rough and strong, and then he drags one of his nails over my nipple. It's a clean, electric sensation. I rub harder. "Not like that."

"The next one," he prompts.

"A guy from my English lit class. He didn't look like you." The detail escapes before I can stop it, and it's too late to get it back. "He liked hand jobs. In the library. He took…" I'm so close. This is torture. He can see everything. "He took forever. And he wouldn't return the favor."

"Look at me." I do, and I can't see my reflection in his eyes but I know what I'd look like. A gasping slut. Red-faced, with messy hair and desperate eyes. Desperate for him. What the hell. What the fuck. Leo smirks. "Those boys didn't deserve you. Take your hand away."

I don't do it, can't do it, and he takes my hand and shoves it out of the way, pinning it to my belly.

And then his dark head is between my thighs.

His mouth is on me.

At first I only have the impression of wet heat, so consuming that my arm gives out and my head falls back on the table. I don't care. I don't care because he presses the flat of his tongue against my clit and it's magic, it's dark magic, it's everything until he seals his mouth over the sensitive nerves. I glimpse heaven. It looks like the night sky and it feels like Leo Morelli's tongue working me over.

Because he doesn't stay, no, he doesn't stay. There is more of me for him to taste and he does it. He gives my slit a long, lingering lick and fucks me with his tongue. My thoughts are on fire, all of them burning up together. Both of his hands dig into my thighs, shockingly hard, and I realize it's because my body has gone crazy. My hips won't stay on the table. They're as desperate as the rest of me.

I open my mouth to beg him to stop, it's too much, it's going to end me, but what comes out instead is a wordless animal noise filled with need and longing. A sob that's not really a sob. Or maybe it is. Either way, he answers it with new focus. In the space of a few heartbeats, he discovers that the thing I can't stand, that the thing driving me right to the edge, is direct attention to my clit. I can't describe what he's doing. I've lost sense of the room. Of the house. Of everything except the pleasure knifing through my belly.

It's a bomb, ticking down to zero. I'm dimly aware of the end approaching because Leo's fingers bruise my thighs. He's strong. He's the strongest man I've ever been with but my body has turned wild enough to challenge him. I get one hand to the tablecloth. Dig my fingers in. Hold on tight. It's coming, it's coming—

A sound vibrates through the glasses on the table. It can't be from me, because I've never made a sound like that. I've never felt pleasure so twisting and huge. My body can't deal with it, can't contain it, and so it doesn't. It frees itself from me in a series of hard shudders, muscles working. The only counterpressure is Leo. He's the one keeping me on earth. I'd die without him. I would.

Luckily he stays where he is, tongue coaxing out a series of smaller aftershocks that bring me down, slowly, slowly. My hands are in his hair. I don't know how they got there. I untangle them with great effort.

"Open your eyes." Leo's big hands lift me to sitting, and I open my eyes on a version of him with tousled hair and wrinkles in his shirt. It was more of a fight to keep me pinned down than I thought. He pushes my hair away from my face. Steadies me on the edge of the table.

He leans back in his chair and the chill in his eyes hauls me back down to the mortifying reality of this moment.

I'm naked on the table. Reduced to a dessert. Leo looks at me the way he would a lopsided cake. He's eaten through the soft parts of me and left nothing behind but the horrible truth that a Morelli—the worst Morelli, the meanest, the cruelest—is the only person ever to make me come so hard I saw the center of the universe.

I find my voice. "Can I go?"

A noise of pure derision. "Go where?"

"To my room?" To lie on the bed and shiver. To cry. I don't know.

"No." He snaps his fingers, pointing down between his knees. "You can get on the fucking floor."

I scramble off the table, heart thundering. The fact that his mouth was on me a minute ago means nothing. Any pleasure I get is a head fake. He threads his fingers into my hair the moment I'm on my knees and yanks me closer until I'm caged in by the frame of his hard thighs.

"Hands behind your back." I obey this, too, while he reaches above my head for something on the table. "I know how much you like to show off your tits."

I don't. I'd say it out loud, but maybe it's not true, because keeping my hands like this does force my breasts out for him and I hate it.

But.

I'm wet.

And it's new heat between my legs, mixing with the juices he left behind.

Leo balances a plate on one muscular thigh. There's cake. There are strawberries. "It's rude to leave before dessert."

He takes one of the strawberries between his fingers and I open my mouth.

Automatically.

He notices.

He laughs.

And then he works the strawberry into my mouth, crushing it against my teeth and tongue until it's a sweet mess running down over my chin. I'm sticky with it by the time he lets me swallow. By the time he moves on to the second strawberry.

This one, he uses to choke me. He makes me open wide, and then he pushes it all the way to the back of my tongue.

"Say *please*."

I do it, around the soft fruit and his hard fingers. He takes his hand away and wipes it across my breast, scraping a nail over my nipple on the way. "Constantines have no table manners. Look at you. Oh, no." He's seen the involuntary jerk of my arms. "Move those hands, and I'll tie them with my belt."

I do not move them.

I stay on my knees, trying to survive this, trying not to be turned on, while Leo Morelli crushes cake in his fingers and coats my tongue with it.

"Fingers back between your legs."

It's too much this time. Too sensitive. Touching it hurts, but there's no way out of this. I agreed to this. I have to do this. He keeps three fingers in my mouth. Too big. Too much. I whimper around them at the first touch.

"You want to be done, don't you?" His voice is level, almost soothing, and I know it's a trick. A trap. "You poor darling. You're a fucking mess, choking on your dessert. I see those tears. Your clit is swollen and it hurts. If I were a nice man, I'd carry you up to your bed and tuck you in." His smile is so dark, it hurts to look at through the sheen of tears I won't let fall.

Leo forces his fingers back. He makes it hard to breathe. "Make yourself come, and you can go upstairs."

Oh, god, I can't. The first swirl of my fingers hurts, and the second one. I'm overstimulated and raw, and I can't breathe around his fingers, and it's humiliating. Degrading. He's right. I'm a mess, my mouth full of sweetness and a deep ache between my legs. I wish he would help me. I rub desperately at my clit. Please, please help me.

He doesn't.

He watches me groan and gasp around his fingers. He watches me struggle to come with dispassionate eyes. He sees the way I'm upright by necessity. I can't lean back. He won't let me. I can't lean forward. I'll gag, and suffocate. My body curves around the raw hurt of my clit and then—

And then—

Pleasure. It's a ragged scrap at first, so entangled with shame that I don't think I'll ever be able to separate the two. My mind keeps going back to him. To the way he touches me. To the way he's touching me now.

It makes me hot.

No prayer in the world can cure me of this

sickness. None. Because the more I rub, the more it hurts, and the better it feels. I want to lean my head against his leg. I want to cry there while I come.

But instead I come on my own fingers, with Leo's eyes burning over my body. I come with a ragged moan, sucking on his fingers against my will. He makes me suck on them until it's over, until the last shudders have come and gone, and then after, until they're clean.

Then he takes his hand away.

I sag to the floor. Air is so wonderful. Every breath is a miracle and a hard slap of a reminder that it happened, it happened, I'll never taste cake again without thinking of this.

"I'm finished with dessert." I look up at him, at the bulge in the front of his pants, at the tension in his jaw. "Time for you to go, darling."

I try to stand, and I'm not halfway to my feet when his hand wraps around my throat with more force than he's ever used before. "I didn't—I'm leaving—"

"Crawl." He drops me to the floor. "All the way upstairs to your room. No tears. Save those for me."

God help me.

I crawl.

CHAPTER THIRTEEN

Haley

NO TEARS. THEY burn at the corners of my eyes. They sting. They threaten and taunt. But they don't fall. No. I don't let them. All the way up to my room. He's left me without clothes again, and that's part of it, isn't it? I fold myself into perfect sheets, turn out the lights, and stare at the ceiling. Part of it is knowing that he has everything, and I have nothing.

I fall asleep thinking about that. Everything. Nothing. Clothes. No clothes. Someone has to pick up my discarded things from the dining room floor. It's not Leo, I'm sure of that. He steps over them with his shining shoes and his expensive clothes and disappears into this enormous building. His bedroom is at the other end of the hall. It feels like a thousand miles.

My dreams are unsteady. One minute my feet are on the deck of a ship and I can't get my balance. The next I'm swimming. The next I'm on dry land, rocks pressing into my soft belly. A shadow above me. A man standing over me. Isn't that always the way? A man, casting his shadow onto your body like he has any right to block the sun.

Or every right to block the sun. To *be* the sun.

Cold, white light wakes me up the next morning. I point my toes under the covers and try to push away how embarrassing this is. The feeling won't be pushed away. Won't be bribed. It digs both heels into my chest and sinks its weight into my bones.

Why do I like what he does to me, even when I hate it?

Why does it make me wet and aching between my legs?

Why, why, why? Pleasure—even twisted pleasure—wasn't part of the contract, but complete access was. And Leo has dug down to the parts of me I didn't think about before. There was no time. There was no space. Now there's nothing but time.

Time to shower. To dry my hair. To decide to leave the robe hanging where it is. I'm not numb. I still feel everything he did to me last night and everything he made me do. Crying would be a relief but his voice whispers *no tears* in my ear and

I can't, I can't.

What I can do is fold myself into the chair by the window and read. Most of my book remained intact. I go back to the first chapter and wait for a box to arrive.

Minutes tick by. Hours. No soft knock at the door. No box. No food. I don't know what to think. He hates me. He pleasured me. Leo is a Morelli and I'm a Constantine, and there can never be any kind of affection between us. He's using me as the means to an end. I'm using him as the means to an end. I don't know which of us is using the other more. Me? Him?

It's enough to give a girl whiplash.

In the early afternoon a tray arrives. Chicken noodle soup, with fat oyster crackers to go with it. I eat my lunch with the book propped in my lap, and then pad back into the bathroom and brush my teeth. It's easiest this way—waiting. I should go and find Leo, but—

He's already found me.

Leo is sitting on the edge of the bed when I come back out. It doesn't matter that I've been waiting for this moment all day. My heart kicks up. Goose bumps roll down my arms. It seemed brave, or nonchalant, to leave the robe in the bathroom. Now it seems foolish. I leave my arms at my sides, aware of every naked inch of me.

He taps something absently against one leg. A leather strap. The same shadows that play over his face from the fading afternoon light slip over the outlines of the strap. I know what that's for. I've been part of enough whispered conversations at school to know. I fold one arm behind my back, nipples peaking. Leo wears all black, tailored black. Expensive. Like he might be going out somewhere soon. Like he might be coming back from somewhere. He even has shoes, and every button, every lace, makes me feel more exposed.

"What the fuck," he says conversationally, "do you think you're doing?"

I know enough to know there's no right answer. "I didn't have clothes, so I stayed in."

His eyes glint. "I should have been more explicit." *Explicit* sounds forbidden in his mouth. Dirty. "You're not some Constantine princess on vacation. There are no more trays to your room, no more sitting here all day. You'll come downstairs whether I'm there or not. Clothes or not."

My cheeks burn with how unfair this is. How wrong of him to do. He toys with me. Humiliates me. I'm out of my mind with it—with how much I hate it, and how much I don't hate it. The sickest, most secret part of me wants to please him. And not just because pleasing him is the only way to save my father. I want that for myself.

"I'm sorry. I'll do better."

Leo stands. "Yes, you will. Bend over the bed."

My heart thrashes inside my rib cage, frantic for a way out, and I lose my grip on being cool. On going along with it. "You didn't say." I clench my fist behind my back. "You didn't say I had to come downstairs, and now you're going to punish me?"

He smirks, eyes lighting up. "You're so fucking cute when you're angry. Yes, I'm going to punish you, but not because you spent the day in your room."

"Then why?"

"Because I like it when you cry."

I grind my teeth together. "Good luck, then."

He moves around the bed and reaches for the remote. The fire blazes to life behind me, bathing the whole room in a heated glow. It makes him look warmer, too, which is cruel. It's the cruelest thing about this moment. In the firelight, Leo is so beautiful that a person could believe he's good. The heat from the fire wraps around me from behind, taunting. If Leo does what I think he'll do, then my skin will do more than burn. It will bruise.

"Already making it worse," he sings. Leo comes back around to the foot of the bed and points to the spot with the strap. "I don't mind, to be clear. But you will."

On leaden legs, conflicted between terror and want, I cross the room and stop at the bed. Bending seems impossible. I'm already naked, already trapped, but bending for him is awful. It's awful, how much I want to do it.

Leather skims across my ass. "I can do it while you're standing, but if you fall, I'll start all over."

I bend.

Leo disappears behind me and kicks my legs apart. This is worse. Yes. This is worse. My heart pounds, my chest beating against the blanket. Each thought freezes into a useless droplet and shatters. Fear closes my throat and makes my knees tremble. I expected pain. Of course I expected pain. He's a Morelli, and they never sign deals that don't hurt. I just couldn't look at this future head-on. I couldn't face it. And now it's happening.

"So you haven't been fucked." Leo slides the strap across my ass. I can't relax, but I can't stay so rigid. "You've only had my fingers in your tight cunt. And the fear in your eyes tells me you've never been punished. That changes now."

He stands to my left, gliding the leather across flesh that's never been strapped. Never been spanked. Hardly touched. My next breath isn't a full one, and the one after that is even less.

It's so fast. Half a heartbeat. The leather lifts away and cracks down in a searing line. I suck in enough air to scream.

Leo laughs. "No, the Constantine brat hasn't been punished." With one foot on mine, he pulls my legs apart again. "Point those toes in. Good girl. You're a natural." The strap cracks again and this time I bite the scream in half. I'm not going to be the one who breaks down like this, not me, not me. "Pretty," he comments. "Red stripes look good on you."

I said I wouldn't cry. I meant it. The covers ball up in my fists.

"I can see you trying not to cry." Leo snaps the belt back again and this time it lights my whole ass on fire. My knees buckle but I don't fall. No sound comes out of my mouth. If I make a sound I'll cry. "No one would be surprised if you went back on your word. It hurts like a motherfucker."

"It does," I hear myself admit, and I also hear

a swallowed sob in my voice. "It hurts so much."

"Point your toes." I have just enough time to register how gently he says it before the words are cut down by a vicious blow. A cry struggles up to my tongue but I keep my lips shut tight, chest heaving.

Leo puts two more lines of fire across my ass, hard and deliberate. I should have known better. I didn't see this particular cruelty coming. I didn't want to see it. A tear breaks free, trickles down my cheek, and lands on the comforter. My toes aren't pointed anymore. He'll strap me again for it. I move myself back into the position and keep hold of the blankets.

"If it's too much, darling, you can leave. Stand up and walk out the door."

The invitation snaps me in two. Breaks me. The tears I've been holding back rush out, soaking the comforter, but I do not stand up. Leo is lying. I can't stand up and leave. I won't. I will do anything for my father, including this. More than this. I will bend over and take whatever depraved punishments Leo Morelli wants to give if it means keeping my dad out of harm's way. There's no stopping the tears now and they run in hot streaks down my face and drip down my nose. I spread my thighs another few inches. Point my toes. "Do it." My voice is rough through the tears. "Hurt me. Do it. I'm not leaving."

One sharp breath. I don't know what it means. Don't turn my head to look. His hand comes from nowhere, and Leo threads his fingers through my hair and pins me to the bed.

For five more strokes.

They last an eternity. Each sharp slap is punctuated by someone crying *please please please* and it's me, it's me, but I don't recognize my own voice. I don't recognize the woman whose hips rock into the bed. Not trying to get away from him, no, trying to feel his hand in my hair, trying to get contact where I need it. A little contact would turn this inside out, turn the breath-stealing pain into something different. It's wrong. It's fucked. I don't care. I can't stop.

Leo puts his fingers between my hip bone and the bed and prompts me up, giving himself enough space to reach between my legs.

Not with his hand.

With the strap.

The one he used to punish me with.

To my horror it feels good on my wet, swollen flesh. I don't know how he's managing to keep it where he wants it, pressing tight against my clit. All that matters is that he does.

"Yes." His voice soothes and humiliates. "Fuck the strap."

My hips jerk against it, senseless, wanting. My tears turn hotter with embarrassment. With the mortification of having to rock my hips into the same leather that made me sob. That made me wet. Leo keeps one hand on my head. It's more intense than being bound, feeling his fingers in my hair. At least, I think it is. He hasn't tied me up yet. An image of myself, panting and coming and restrained, makes me work myself harder against the strap.

"Come, or we can start over."

He means he'll take the wet strap from between my legs and punish me with it again, right here, right now. Leo would do it. He would degrade me with a strip of leather soaked in my own juices, he would laugh at my tears, he would—he would—

I come so hard my knees give out and my vision dims. From the distant reaches of space, I try to keep myself upright. Try to keep my legs spread. He'll fuck me now. That's the logical conclusion of all this. He'll take my virginity while my ass burns and my tears flow and I make these sounds, god, I can't stop.

Leo tugs the strap out from under me. It

comes free with a wet, slick sound.

I sense the motion rather than see it and half-brace for the final blow. It knocks my soul from my body, sends my mind spinning into nothing.

My sob turns into a moan, and I fall down onto my knees, my hands on the edge of the bed.

A moan.

Jesus.

Leo picks me up from where I've fallen and drops me unceremoniously onto the bed. I can't see through tears, through the haze of pain and orgasm. He's a dark tear in the fabric of my world. He's headed for the door. I roll over onto my side. Push myself up. "Don't go," I manage.

It's too late. He's already gone.

CHAPTER FOURTEEN

Haley

THE PART THAT surprises me is the clarity.

My ass hurts. The pain sticks around. It settles into an ache, rather than a sharp snap. I don't feel like sleeping. When I'm sure he's not coming back I ease myself off the bed and go to check the damage in the bathroom mirror.

No bruises. Just redness over my ass and thighs. The strapping felt worse than it was. A person would have to be skilled, in order to do that. To hurt only as much as they intended.

And it was intentional. I rub my hands over the marks Leo left, that strange, clear feeling arranging my thoughts into an understandable pattern. He's scary, yes, but he's also trying to scare me. He goes out of his way to keep me off-balance. He never gives me solid ground.

There are characters like that in my favorite books. Their cruelty is a shield for a dark secret, like a wife hidden in an attic.

I splash water on my face, Leo's voice echoing in my head. There was something he said. Thinking of it now makes hairs rise on the back of my neck. The feeling of it—the truth of it. With my face buried in a hand towel I can hear it.

It hurts like a motherfucker.

He didn't say *it must hurt.*

He said *it hurts.*

I meet my eyes in the mirror. Now I have two questions about Leo Morelli. Who hurt him, and what is he hiding?

The two things have to be related.

Back in the bedroom, my clothes wait for me on the foot of the bed. The lingerie is missing but there's a new bra-and-panty set. It all smells like fabric softener. Mrs. Page must have come in and dropped them off. Leo must have told her to do it. It would have been meaner to make me go without clothes.

No solid ground.

I get dressed and go out into the hall, not bothering to stop and listen for anyone else. He's hiding something. He's hiding from *me.* I'm going to find him and ask. A reckless plan? Yes. Yes. But I have a clear head and I want to know, damn it.

Something stops me outside the big door that

goes into his bedroom. What did Mrs. Page say? His rooms. A suite, then. I listen at the door. No sound comes from inside, but…

I put a hand on the doorknob. This is as good a place to start looking as any, if it's unlocked.

It is.

The enormous door opens into an equally enormous room.

Leo's bedroom.

Vaulted ceilings remind me of a cathedral, and so does the polished darkness here. Gleaming wood paneling. Thick, dark rugs. It feels like a fortress. Leo has his own fireplace, more massive in scale than any of the others. I'm going to ask him about the fireplaces someday. Were they original to the house? It would make sense, if this is a historical property. People needed lots of them for heat. The mantel looks original, if redecorated.

Enormous windows look out over the night-kissed grounds. Distant trees are black silhouettes against a navy sky dotted with stars. Pure, clean snow.

And in front of the windows, the bed.

The bed grabs my attention with both hands. He sleeps here. It's hard to imagine him sleeping. The strap Leo used on me has been abandoned on the comforter. It's a few inches from the far side of the mattress, like he threw it there on his way to somewhere else.

I'm so busy looking at it and trying to ignore the pulsing heat between my legs that I don't hear the water running at first.

In my house, it's impossible to miss running water. It's too small a space, and the plumbing is too old. Not like it is here. In Leo's house, the sound of a shower is barely audible.

Loud enough for me to follow.

A hallway takes me further into the room, past two doors on either side. One reveals a walk-in closet the size of our living room at home. One is closed. I keep going. The hall opens into the front corner of the house. All windows here. All light. A view of the circle drive. There's a sitting area here with an overstuffed chair. Two books are stacked on a side table nearby.

I don't look at them.

The rest of the space is a personal library. It dead-ends into a wall with floor-to-ceiling shelves, a writing desk, and an armchair big enough for someone as tall as Leo to be comfortable in.

A pair of doors set into the inner wall must lead to the same space as the closed door from the hall. That's where the running water is coming from.

Judging by the space carved out by these walls, Leo's bathroom is bigger than the guest bathroom. It's bigger than most Constantine bathrooms I've seen.

But the size is not the thrill.

The thrill is knowing that Leo is in the shower behind those doors. I wouldn't go so far as to say he invited me here, but he didn't *not* invite me. He had someone leave my clothes in case I got up. He knows I'm in the house.

I take a deep breath and open the first door.

The shower is louder in here, but not visible. What is visible is a soaking tub surrounded by the same stone tiles that dominate the rest of the space, a low bench nearby. The tiles warm my feet. Heated floors. He really does have everything, including a double sink with real cabinet space and an open linen closet stocked with rolled towels and neat bottles of shampoo and conditioner and soap.

An archway leads into the shower room. I'm determined now. I need at least one of his secrets to make sense of him. I can't do that if I'm hiding in my room. I can't hide in my room anymore, either. Leo's forbidden it. My ass smarts under my clothes.

The approach to the archway gives me enough time to be nervous. I reach for the stonework of the arch and move into the opening.

Leo's shower is the fanciest thing I have ever seen. A wooden bench runs along one glassed-in wall. The other side is taken up with stone shelves, all the angles smoothed out. Designed that way on purpose. The water runs straight down over him, like rain.

My breath stops at the sight. Water runs over his hair and catches in it, diamond-like and glistening. It runs over strong shoulders, strong arms, the arms he braced to keep my legs apart, and down over—

My whole body jolts as his back registers in a series of shocks, each one its own punch to the gut.

His back is a mess of scars. Angry, obvious scars. There are so many that I don't know where to look first. His hands are in his hair but his shoulders are tense in a way that seems wrong for a shower this nice. My heart turns over, tries to run. It had to have hurt. That many scars, that much pain, it can only be from…what? A car accident?

My mind supplies the answer in a horrified whisper. No. Not an accident. He was whipped.

I must make some sound, because his head comes up.

He turns.

He sees me.

I stumble back a step from the incandescent shock and fury on his face. He's not hiding any of it, and I was wrong. I was wrong to think he was angry at dinner. I didn't know what that looked like, and now I do. I wish I didn't.

"What the fuck are you doing in here?" His body is a storm, and his voice is a lash of lightning on aching flesh.

I put a hand back on the arch for balance. Oh, god, oh, god. "Who did that to you?"

His eyes darken. They're the color of blackened wood. The color of a house fire. The color of rage.

He storms out of the shower, dripping wet, beautiful and unholy. A scream stops itself in my throat. He fists my hair, digging his fingers in hard, and tips my face up to his. Water drips onto my dress. He's breathing fast, like he's been running, and it strikes me even now that he'd be magnificent running. Everything about him is magnificent and fucking terrifying. Water from his hand works its way into my hair.

"You think," Leo grits his teeth, "you think

you can come in here, and what? I'll strap your ass and lick your clit again? Are you that fucking horny? You're here to service me, not the other way around."

He drags me backward through the archway, into the open space. I reach for his fist in my hair on instinct but he bats my hand away, then pulls my face back to his.

"If you're so hot for it, get down on your knees."

Leo doesn't wait for me to answer. Doesn't wait for anything. He has me by the hair and he pushes me down, onto the floor. I'm a heartbeat and nothing else. I'm fear and a sick, twisted want and nothing else. Leo works his thumb between my teeth and opens my mouth.

He's hard. And huge.

It occurs to me now that he was hard when I first saw him in the shower. He was thinking about something that turned him on. Me?

He strokes down his length with his free hand, his thumb on my tongue. "Have you ever sucked cock before?"

I shake my head no. I don't dare close my mouth.

"Good." He says it like a condemnation, but I hear approval, or I want to hear approval.

And then there's no more time to think.

Leo shoves his cock into my mouth without preamble. Without hesitation. One heartbeat I'm waiting, dying of the wait, and the next he's filling my mouth. Water drips from his skin onto my hair and my dress but I hardly feel it. I can't feel anything but his hands twisting in my hair and the impossible length of him taking all the available space.

Choking me.

I gag on him and he pulls back with a biting laugh, reaching around to swipe a tear from my cheek. He pulls my head back so I can see him licking the salt off his thumb, and then he grips my hair for leverage to fuck my mouth.

To use it.

Like it belongs to him.

"Suck."

I know in my heart that there are no second chances with this. No boundary he won't cross if I screw this up. I scramble for anything to hold on to and find his hard thighs.

I suck.

I try my best to use my tongue. He's hard but his skin is so soft. Experimentally I trail my tongue along the underside of his cock and his body bends forward, his grip loosening in my hair. I get more of his hand around the back of my head. Less of his cruel grip. Cruel or not, he controls me completely. I do it again and get a grunt that's part pleasure and mostly pain, and somewhere, underneath the panic of trying not to gag on him and the startling lack of air, the intimacy of this becomes so clear it hurts.

"Swallow."

Another flash of panic lights up the dark sky of me. If he's going to come—

He's not.

I swallow just in time to figure out that what he means is to take him deep. Too deep. It's killing me. I can't do this. He strokes into my throat with abandon and I'm fighting him, clawing at him—

Only I'm not clawing. I'm pulling him closer, my hands hooked around the backs of his legs, and nothing is more fucked up than this. Nothing, nothing, nothing.

Except the way I want him. Except the way my whole body is reacting to being demeaned like this. Used like this. Hurt like this. My skin is on fire with the need to know him, to wring the truth out of him, to come out of this with more than a sacrifice. I'll give myself to Leo to save my dad but I want to take part of him too.

Leo pulls out so abruptly that I fall forward, hands hitting the floor with a loud slap. I can't catch my breath. I struggle for it, and struggle, and struggle. Finally it returns.

So does Leo.

He pulls me back to my knees with a hand under my jaw, his cock in his fist, stroking it while he looks into my eyes. Tears leak from the corners but I'm not crying. I'll be crying soon if I don't get to come. I'll be crying soon if there's nowhere for the slick need between my legs to go.

I inch closer to him and brush my lips over the head of his cock. He groans and gives me an inch. I swirl my tongue around it and he gives me another one. This is the most depraved begging I've ever done, and Leo is wound tight around it. He feeds me inch after inch until something in him snaps.

His hands go back to my hair and his muscles work under my palms. Working to hold him upright. Working to keep him standing. He says something that I don't hear over the rush of blood in my ears, the beating fear that I'm choking, I'm choking, and then he surges forward and comes.

Hard.

I can either drown or swallow and instinct takes over. He tastes like salt and hurt. At some point it peaks and his hands gentle in my hair, both hands pulling me close, one sliding down to the back of my neck.

When he's spent he pulls out, but he keeps his hands where they are. I rest my forehead against his thigh and breathe. The air has never felt so good in my lungs. Leo's running his fingers through my hair in an absent way, like he's still floating. A quiet warning sounds in the back of my mind. I know. I know. This isn't over. I can't take back what I've seen. I know. But I don't want to let go.

His breathing settles. And the warning gets louder.

I stay on my knees.

CHAPTER FIFTEEN

Leo

I COME BACK to my body. A cage of flesh and pain. My return is abrupt.

And it.

Is.

Agony.

I have my hands in her hair, her soft, spun-gold hair, and the way she's touching me—like I didn't just hold her by that hair and fuck her throat until tears ran down her cheeks, like I didn't punish her for no other reason than I wanted to—is gentle and intimate and unbearable.

What am I doing? What the fuck have I been doing?

Anger and pain collide in a black, roaring storm and I wrench my hands away from her hair like they've been burned. They are burning. To touch Haley is to be flayed alive. She saw. She's here. She fucking saw.

SECRET BEAST

Haley scrambles backward, an animal caught in a hunter's beam, and it should make me feel sorry for her but those huge, innocent eyes are oxygen to flame. A lit match to gasoline. I hate that she's here. I hate that she saw. This rage is too large to be contained, too big for muscle and bone to keep in. I hear myself snarl and she startles, getting up to her feet, staying low. As if that could save her.

I'm beyond saving.

I'm so fucking pissed that it's acid on open wounds, and at the middle is a secret, desperate humiliation that I will do anything to shake loose.

Haley is frozen, one hand up, showing me the whites in her eyes. "I'm sorry." Her voice trembles. "I didn't know—I'm sorry."

I reach one hand out before she can run and coil my fingers through her hair, hard enough that she yelps, her face contorting with pain. "You're not sorry enough." My voice sounds nightmarish even to me, and Haley flinches at the sound. "The strap wasn't enough to teach you your place, was it? No, it fucking wasn't." Haley comes with me when I leave the bathroom. She doesn't have any choice. My grip is so tight in her hair that she can't breathe. She struggles to get her feet under her.

171

"Leo." It's a begging gasp and it yanks at something far under the surface of me. Beneath the torn skin and the scrambled nerves. Deeper. Older. "Please." In the bedroom I let her fall next to the bed. She gets up, eyes wide, the color drained from her face. I'm between her and the door. She could try to climb backward but there's no way she makes it. Haley holds up both hands. "We could talk about it. You're—" Fast breathing. Hard breathing. She's cornered and ready to run. "You're hurt—"

"No." Haley snaps her lips closed, lifting her chin to keep her eyes on me. I'm so close I can feel her heartbeat through the air. This is how you hide the things that eat you alive. You crowd in. Take up all the space. No one can see your secrets if they're hidden behind power and rage. "I'm not hurt. But I'm going to hurt you. You want to know what it's like? I'll show you. I'll whip you hard enough to leave scars. Hard enough to bleed."

It's not true. I don't mean it. A person like Haley, who sobs from a strapping and blushes when it makes her wet, could not survive what happened to me. Wouldn't survive. She would live but she wouldn't survive. It would break her.

I won't whip her. But fuck, I want to hurt

her. I want to make her cry. I want to give in to the monstrous humiliation that squeezes my muscles in its fists and stops my heart. How dare she. How fucking dare she.

"Okay," she whispers, her face the picture of pain and fear and everything I should want out of a Constantine. "Okay. If that's what you have to do. Okay, okay." One tear slips down her cheek, then another. Haley's shoulders shake. The urge to fuck her is as strong as the urge to hurt her. I want them both.

The sweet, crying Constantine lifts her hands and puts them on my chest. Flat. Soft. No nails, no fight. I'm not calmed, no, fuck no. But I feel closer to the ground.

I take a step back.

Haley bolts.

On instinct I reach for her, my fingertips brushing fabric, but she's fast. The door to my rooms is already open and she goes through. For the first time in years, I can't move. Anger has settled into my cells, radioactive and heavy. It clouds my mind. Makes my jaw hurt. Makes my back hurt and hurt and hurt. Nerve pain I can't shake.

I should go after her before she causes a scene in the household. There's been enough drama for one night. Enough bullshit. Enough of these emotions, which have teeth and claws.

The one thing I can't do, even in my own home, is go after her without clothes. It pisses me off all over again.

"Fuck you," I say to the empty air as I stalk into my closet. I don't know who I'm saying it to.

✧ ✧ ✧

Haley

I'M USED TO swallowing fear and its lesser cousin, nervousness. How could I not be? I'm a Constantine who is not a Constantine. I never know how people will react when I walk into a room. Some of them are disapproving, verging on dangerous, like Aunt Caroline. Some of them never bother to look twice. Some of them dig and dig and dig until they finally find out I'm not that kind of Constantine. Not the kind with money or status. But I have the name, so I could be useful.

This terror can't be swallowed. I'd choke on it, and I'd die.

Leo might have meant what he said. That's the big fear, the one that has me running down the stairs in bare feet, my hand grazing the railing. He's capable of whipping a person until they bleed. I know that. Everyone knows that. He's capable of every dark and terrible thing. But that's not why I'm gasping, unable to catch my breath, holding in more sobs.

It's because of what I saw in his eyes.

Shattered glass. A shattered heart. A dark well brimming with hurt, and at the bottom—shame. Leo wasn't only angry at me for being in a place I wasn't supposed to be. He was furious that I saw a secret he's been trying to keep for long enough that it's cut him up on the inside.

It hurts him so much. It's impossible to judge the size of what *it* is, to judge the contours. All I know is that his secret is a kind of torture, and a person in that much pain will do anything to make it stop.

I reach the bottom of the steps, turn blindly to the right, and collide with Mrs. Page, who has a neat stack of clothing in her arms. Clothing that looks like it's for me. I take a pair of socks off the top and put them on.

"Haley?" Her worried eyes meet mine when I straighten up. "What—"

"Where is the door to the garage?"

Her mouth drops open. "Miss Constantine, I can't—"

Panic body-checks me and slithers its way down my arms to my hands. I grab for Mrs.

Page's shoulders and shake her. "Tell me where to go. Now. Right now."

Mrs. Page takes a step back and gestures down the hall behind her. "A left at the end of the hall. There's a passageway that goes through—"

I don't stop to listen to the rest. I've never been to the end of this hallway, but once I'm there, I see it doesn't end. A hallway winds through to an outer door that is blessedly not locked. It opens under my frantic push and I hurry through another hall built from stones and set with narrow windows. On the other side a door leads into Leo's cavernous garage.

I was right, that first night I arrived. There are more than four cars. There are nine, counting mine, tucked all the way at the end in front of one of the doors. A panel on the wall has easy enough buttons. I hit one and the door in front of my car lifts.

A hundred silent prayers race through my brain while I run. Please, let the keys be in the car. Please, let him not be chasing me. Please, please, please. The first thing I do is pop the trunk. Wedged all the way in the back are a pair of rain boots I had for a mandatory horticulture class. A brisk wind whips in as I pull them on. Better than nothing. Better than staying.

The keys are in the ignition and the car comes to life without hesitation.

I sag over the steering wheel. "Thank you," I whisper to the car.

Which makes me think of Leo.

Which makes me put the car in drive and gun it out of the garage.

The final obstacle is the gate, and I accelerate toward it and hold my breath. Believe. Believe that it's going to open. Believe that I can survive this if I have to crash through it and run. I believe.

It opens.

I sail through, almost let down by how easy it was.

A fresh layer of powder covers the center line, and I concentrate so hard on driving that it takes me several miles to notice the lack of snowflakes inside the car. Someone must have been working on it. Leo must have had someone working on it. I shake my head and turn up the radio. No thinking about him now. Not when my heart is out of its mind.

I follow the light pollution to the highway, and the highway to the city, and the city's edge to the same road where all of this started. I'm three blocks past the alley where I first met Leo when the car shudders.

"Not now," I tell it, and pat the wheel. "Not now. We have to get home first."

It shudders again, and dread turns my stomach.

"No, no, no." I don't have a coat. I don't have a purse. I don't have anything, and if this car dies, I will be so, so screwed. It's nighttime at the wharf. My hair is standing on end.

The car whines, rising into a shriek, and the wheel jerks in my hands. It's unsteady now, all wrong noises and a hard rattle that makes my teeth snap together. I make it to the side of the road and throw the driver's side door open.

Screaming into the steering wheel will not fix this. The only thing that will fix this is walking until I find a place that will let me borrow a phone. Jesus, it's cold. The wind is made from blades that grab at my dress and tear at my skin. Going across the street at least gets me some mild protection from the gusts. I'm not much of a runner, but I break into a jog. The air is so cold it hurts—or I'm used to Leo's house, which seemed cold at first, cold and forbidding, but is actually warm. It's so warm.

I do not want to go back.

I don't.

My teeth chatter. All the stores I pass are dark,

but there will be a bodega or a café or somewhere with a person inside. Someone will have a cell phone. Somehow I'll call my family, and they will come to get me, and I will be warm and safe and—

A hand shoots out of an alley, barring my path. I run straight into it. The fist wraps around the front of my dress and pulls me into an alley. "Hey." I try to dislodge the hand, but he's holding on tight. "Hey. Stop."

"*You* stop." The man grins. "Girls running down the street like that have to stop and see us. We're in charge of this block, and we don't let people go through without a chat."

I grab his wrist in both hands and twist at it, my stomach sinking. I don't remember. I don't remember the self-defense class I took my freshman year. I don't remember how to use his weight as leverage. My nails are all I have, and I dig them into the skin of his wrist.

"Bitch," he spits, and then his arm is around my neck, my back to his chest, and he's dragging me farther back into the shadows.

There are three of them, here in the alley, and the first one presses his arm tight to my neck. It's not the easy, controlled grip Leo has. This man means to scare me. He means to kill me. My hands scrabble at his arm but he doesn't let go. Can't breathe. Can't get a breath. No, no. Getting dark, dark, dark—

He throws me down onto the ground. The frigid cold shocks me back to life in time for the other two to step over me. One reaches down to pin my arms above my head. Oh my god. Oh my god. My brain disconnects from the sopping, freezing cold of the dirty slush underneath me and I wrench my wrists free and kick out. One of them tries to kick me back. I avoid it by rolling, which soaks the rest of my clothes. It makes them laugh. So does getting to my feet.

One of them steps in close. Adrenaline is a silvery rush in my veins and I shove him as hard as I can and sprint for the open end of the alley. Strong arms lock around my waist and a scream tears out of me. If they take me to the darkest corner, I'm dead. A beam of light cuts across the opening of the alley. A streetlight. God. A streetlight in this shitty part of New York City is the last thing I'm going to see before they put me back on the ground.

A silhouette punches through the light, storming into the alley with a snarl that echoes off the bricks and pummels us. I freeze in place, and the man's arms tighten—

And let go.

You don't stand still in the presence of a natural disaster, and what's stalking toward us now is worse than a natural disaster.

It's Leo.

I get flashes of bared teeth and burning eyes. A tall, hard body in black clothes. And in his hand, the metallic glint of a knife.

A knife. He has a *knife*.

Leo doesn't stop for me. Doesn't look down at me to search my eyes for proof I'm all right. He swings out one arm and pushes me toward the mouth of the alley.

I make it two steps, and then I turn back.

The men are cornered now. It's three on one, but Leo seems larger than life. Faster. Stronger. I bite back a warning. Warn who? The men? They know who came for them. They all talk at once, voices crashing into one another and becoming senseless noise.

They don't stand a chance. They would have stood a better chance if Leo had called the police, but of course he didn't. He's a law unto himself.

The first one goes down with a scream. The other two split up. Go different directions. Leo catches one of them around the collar. He reaches around and stabs the man in the back, and that man dies with an arched spine and a rattling breath.

Leo doesn't spare him a second glance. He turns and runs. I'm right. He is magnificent in motion. A deadly weapon. I turn around and watch him use the corner of the building to launch himself onto the sidewalk.

The last man must have been running fast.

Not fast enough.

The two of them reappear as more silhouettes, the man kicking and shouting, Leo dragging him by the back of his jacket. The man gets his feet under him and shoves, and the two of them end up by the alley wall.

Leo's on the outside, the man backed against the bricks, and the rush of blood is so loud in my head I can't hear what he's saying. Can't be certain where either of their hands are. Leo shakes him, slamming the man's head back against the brick, and it's a distraction. It was always meant to be a distraction from his other hand, which is down low with the knife.

Twisting.

Twisting.

Twisting.

The man who had his hands on me, who was dragging me back toward certain death, dies with his own blood spilling out of his mouth and onto the front of his shirt. Leo stands over his prey while the body coughs up its last breath. I think Leo's saying something. I can't be sure. Then he turns from the corpse like it's nothing.

My shivers have turned violent, uncontrollable, and oh—how about that. I can't move. Leo strides toward me with the easy confidence of a seasoned killer. I don't see what he does with the knife. It's gone by the time he reaches me.

"Is it over?" Each word is broken into pieces by chattering teeth.

Expression unreadable, Leo steps to my side and puts a hand on my arm. He guides me out of the alley, where a black SUV waits at the curb. Leo heads toward it. He didn't even stop to turn off the headlights. He ran for me. Killed for me. Why?

"Leo." He pulls open the passenger door of the SUV and pauses, looking down at me. Maybe his face isn't blank. Maybe it's concealing something. There's a difference. "You came for me. You killed those men."

A huff. "Get in the fucking car."

CHAPTER SIXTEEN

Haley

ALL THE FIGHT goes out of me in the passenger seat of Leo's SUV. The adrenaline runs away like that last man he killed, only the heart-hammering rush makes a successful escape. Leo tosses something over me. The heavy wool of his overcoat. I steal a glance at him as he puts the car in drive and accelerates away from the alley.

I've seen him in a sweater. I've seen him in a dress shirt. I can imagine how he'd look in a full suit with a jacket. Leo doesn't wear any of that now. An equally dark shirt clings to his arms and torso. Dark gloves. Dark hat. It looks natural on him. He's at ease haunting people's fears.

Those men in the alley will never dream again.

I wrap myself into Leo's coat. It's soft the way expensive things are soft. Solid the way expensive things are solid. It can't stop my shivering.

Leo drives us down the road, buildings and

alleys passing by in a haze, until he pulls to the curb. I peek at him over the collar of his coat. His eyes are so dark in the glow from the center console. So endless. He's hidden the pain and rage again. Forced it back under a layer of something I can't put a name to.

"Do you remember the strap, darling?"

My body convulses from another set of shivers. "Yes."

"I'll make it twice as bad if you step one foot outside." Leo reaches over me and opens the glove box. Pulls something out. Slams it shut. For a brief second I think he might touch me, but he doesn't. He gets out of the car and strides across the empty street to an alley. Inside that alley, a fire burns inside a trash can. The sight of it makes bile burn my throat. So many alleys. So many men. Dead men, now. I can't think about their bodies falling or I'll lose it.

There are a few men huddled around the metal garbage bin and Leo waves them away. They scatter like rats, backing up into the dark. Leo steps up to the fire and strips off his shirt and gloves and hat. All of it goes into the flames. He tugs another shirt on. Oh—the shirt from the glove box.

I'm not scared for him when he turns his back

on those men. I'm not scared for me. He's far more dangerous than I thought. He's saved me twice. The contradiction doesn't leave room for anything but the struggle to get warm.

"Why didn't you shoot them?" I feel compelled to ask this. Conversation will pass the time, and I want to know. The more I think about Leo's tall, hard body in that alley, the more I have to understand why.

He scoffs. "Those men didn't deserve the mercy of a bullet through the head." Leo's a good driver, his hands steady on the wheel. I feel safe right now. "And guns are a coward's way out. If you're going to kill someone, do it with your eyes open."

It happens on the way back to his house. The heat wraps around the coat, and I can't keep my eyes open. I drift in and out and only wake up when a gust of cold wind hits me from the open door of the SUV.

Leo leans in over me, undoes my seat belt, and swings my legs out of the car. "Can you walk?"

"Yes." A frisson of offense. "Of course I can."

"When I found you tonight, you couldn't run." He wraps an arm around me and the coat and hurries me up the front steps. We go through the front door. I trip over the rubber toe of one of my boots, but with my hands in the overcoat I can't catch myself. He catches me instead, bundling me up into his arms with an irritated sigh. "This time, so we're clear, you're staying where I put you. Not fucking off to the city and getting yourself killed."

"I didn't get killed." He turns at the top of the stairs, and I think he's going to take me to the guest room. I brace for it. But instead he shoulders open the door to his bedroom and goes inside. Leo deposits me on my feet at the foot of the bed. "Why are we in here?"

"Your clothes are wet." He disappears from view. "And filthy. Come on."

It has to be a trap. It wasn't very long ago that he threatened me with a severe whipping for going this way without permission. But my skin prickles with the need to stay near him. As close as possible.

Leo emerges from his closet with an armful of clothes and goes down the hall without looking back. I follow him into the bathroom. Water rushes into the tub and he sits on the edge, a hand dipped in to test the warmth. He shakes off the droplets with an assessing look at me. Then he comes back and works his hands quickly over my clothes. The overcoat falls in a heap. The dress next. My shoes. Leggings. Everything. Then he walks me over to the tub with his hands on my shoulders and helps me step inside.

"This isn't like you," I say, from somewhere outside my body.

"Please. I don't let filth inside my house. On your knees."

A shameful heat echoes between my legs, but when I'm up on my knees in the tub, Leo doesn't put his fingers in my mouth or order me to suck him off or any of the infinite dirty things he could do.

He washes my hair. He conditions it. He presses a washcloth into my hand so I can clean my skin. Under other circumstances I'd float in this tub forever. Now I want the water off me. I want it to go down the drain and take the fingerprints of those men with it. At the end of the bath Leo unfolds a towel and holds it wide, and I step into it. There. There. It's over. That part is over, at least. He lets me fold it over my chest and tuck it in.

I run a hand over my wet hair. "I bet you don't have a brush in here." Leo stands in the middle of his bathroom. Dark jeans. Dark shirt. And a darker patch on the front of that shirt that has a strange shine to it. My heart stutters. "Is that blood?" He changed his shirt. He threw the original shirt in the fire. This is a new one. "Is that yours?"

Leo glances down at the front of his shirt. A ginger touch to the darker spot. His fingers come away red. "One of them had a knife. I wasn't paying much attention to it."

"Oh my god." I go to him without thinking and reach for the hem of his shirt. His hand comes down hard on mine, his eyes blazing, but I shake it off. "Leo, let me see. You're bleeding. You're hurt."

"It's a scratch. I don't even feel it."

Those words sound true, in his strong, clear voice. But I look into his dark eyes and see he's lying.

It's a wretched lie. A lie he wishes he didn't have to tell. Because he does feel it. The gold streaks in his eyes are bright with pain. So bright it takes my breath away. My heart tips onto the floor and breaks like a delicate vase. He feels this pain and all his past pain. Leo Morelli is a tuning fork of pain. It runs through him in such jagged vibrations that the only way to look directly at it is to pretend it's anger. If you see it for what it is—

God.

I draw myself up to my full height. "Sit down. You shouldn't be standing."

His eyes flutter closed for a bare instant, and the broken pieces of my heart burst apart again. He follows me to the bench by his tub and sits, his jaw tight.

I knot the towel more securely around my chest. "I have to take your shirt off to see." He gives a terse nod and another layer of pretense falls away. The cloth of his shirt is stuck to his skin in the front. Leo braces his hands on the side of the tub and grits his teeth. "I'll be fast."

Leo hisses when I pull the fabric away from his skin, his whole body tensing. He helps me get the shirt over his head. I drop it to the floor. Leo puts his hands back on the edge of the tub and stares at the ceiling.

The cut isn't as deep as I feared, but it's longer—a slash. "Do you think we should go to the—"

"No," he barks. "Are you fucking kidding me?" I glare at him, and he glares back, but it doesn't last. His face softens. "I'm not going to any hospital in the city. People will talk."

I'm guessing that means he doesn't trust anyone to come to him, either. A beast doesn't need civilized things like doctors and hospitals. He'd only go if he had no other choice. "Okay. Do you have a first aid kit?"

"Top shelf of the closet."

I find it, then come back with towels and washcloths. I kneel next to him on the bench and lean into the tub to run more warm water. Leo makes a low sound.

"What?"

"Your towel's coming off."

It is. It's almost halfway off one breast. "Thank you," I tell him.

For the first time, he doesn't sneer, or taunt. I dip a clean washcloth in warm water, then settle onto the bench next to him. "I don't think you'll need stitches, but we should clean it."

"Do it, then." Leo's knuckles go white on the edge of the tub. An ache drills itself into my chest. I wish I could cry to untwist that knot, but it seems wrong to cry. Disingenuous.

He's the one in pain, not me, and it's sketched in every tense angle of his muscles. He doesn't let his back make contact with the stones. It's so subtle, the way he keeps his skin from touching. So obvious to anyone who bothers to look. My heart beats like soft, frantic wings in an erratic pattern. I've never been this close to him. Not like this.

"Haley," he says, and I could cry.

I brush my fingers over the curve of his shoulder, where there are no scars. "Is this okay?"

Another nod.

"I'm going to start here, then." Direct pressure on the wound would be too much. I can tell from the stretched-tight tension in every single line of Leo's body. One more dip in the warm water, and then I press it to that spot on his shoulder and rub in gentle circles.

A person bracing for pain will feel more pain. I don't want that for him. I curve my hand over the washcloth and slide it down to his bicep.

His shoulders let down a little. Leo says something under his breath, so quiet I can't make out the words. I don't ask.

I repeat the process on the other side. Slow, even breaths. No shaking hands. I'm too far past his defenses for any wrong move. Leo breathes, his eyes closed, dark eyelashes skimming his cheeks. One fist opens, flexes, closes again. I take his hand in mine and move it to my waist. If he asks why, I'll tell him that it's because I want him to be able to feel what I'm doing.

I will not tell him that it's because his hand there steadies me, too.

Fresh water on the washcloth. I put it on his shoulder above the wound and his hand tightens on my waist. "Just my hand." I lift the washcloth away and bring it back, slowly, slowly, and press it against the broken skin with the flat of my hand. Leo hisses, turning his face away. Rivulets of blood run down from underneath the washcloth. I can feel the wild thrash of his heart. "One more time." More water. The lightest pressure I can manage. His jaw works and my heart leaps outside my body. I wish it was easier. I wish, I wish.

The bleeding is less when I take the washcloth away, and then it's time for a dry towel. Leo's eyes catch mine the moment before I lay it over his skin and some inner part of me collapses. He doesn't show fear, but sometimes it flashes through his eyes anyway. "Hold it there while I get the Neosporin."

He laughs, anguish in the sound. "Why bother?"

I'm already rummaging through the first aid kit, plucking out a long bandage with a soft center, some gauze, and yes, the Neosporin. "So you don't get a blood infection and die."

"You're right. The second one would probably kill me."

I return to the business of taking off the towel and dispensing Neosporin. Leo puts his hand back on my waist. "Second? I thought Morellis had invincible blood."

"They don't."

I hold up one hand so he can see it. Leo pulls me closer. I pretend the heat of the bathroom makes me blush and not his reflex. I pretend with all my might. "I'm sorry," I say into his ear, and then I skim the cream over the wound.

Another hiss, and Leo pulls his entire arm in close, me along with it. He stays that way for several heartbeats before he can begin to relax.

"Gauze," I narrate, trying to hurry without screwing it up. "Bandage. Done."

I expect him to let go. To push me away, even. But Leo's head is bowed, his eyes closed. His lips move but I can't make out what he's saying.

In the absence of knowing what to do, I put a hand on the back of his neck. "Is it the cut? Because if it is, maybe there's someone we can call."

"The cut is fine. You fixed it." His voice sounds ready to snap.

I keep my hand where it is. "How long have you had the scars?"

The noise he makes is meant to be a laugh, but it's tight and tortured. Leo holds me closer. I don't know if he's aware he's doing it. "When I was fourteen, there was an older woman." Cold horror spreads through the pit of my stomach. Fourteen. That's too young. I must stiffen, because Leo barks another laugh. "Yeah. Fourteen. She came on to me. Seduced me. At first I thought it was pretty hot."

I stroke the back of his neck. Gentle. Gentle. Please, let this thing not have happened to him. But it did. Pain streaks across his face, and he rearranges his expression. An old habit.

"Then she started to get…" A pause. A search. "Psycho. So I decided to end it. I told her it was over, and she cried. The smile––" He shudders. "She smiled while she was crying. *One last time, baby.* It was an obvious trick." Leo takes a sharp breath. "She tied me up and whipped me to punish me, and prove her point."

He doesn't have to describe any more. The scars are visible evidence.

"Thought I might die, but I didn't. I dragged myself home and let Eva patch me up. My sister. She was standing in the fucking foyer, otherwise I wouldn't have told her either."

It sounds like a lie. I think he would have told his sister. But I don't interrupt, because the story isn't over.

"I made her help me hide it from the rest of

the family. Then it got infected. She's the one who took me to the hospital and back home again after."

The way he says *hospital* makes it sound bad. Unresolved. I run my fingers through his hair, then down over his neck, careful as I've ever been in my life not to touch any lower, where there are scars. "And it still hurts you, even now."

"No. It feels great." Another hiss, as clear and pained as it was when I cleaned his cut. He's trembling with unreleased tension and hurt. "I don't know if it was the whipping or the infection but my nerves are all fucked up. Stress can set it off, or touch…"

"Should I stop—"

"No," he growls, and then his hand comes up to cover mine, pinning it to the back of his neck. One deep breath. Then another. And another. It grips him, this pain, in big, huge fists. I'm terrified it will last forever. Fear beats in my blood along with my pulse, but then it seems to peak. Leo takes another breath. Opens his eyes. Straightens. "Fuck."

A long silence.

"I swore never to trust a woman again. Or anyone. And I swore I would get revenge."

He hasn't released me, but he pats at my hand

on his neck and drops his hand to his side. "Of course you did. It's awful." My voice almost breaks. "That's awful, what happened to you. I understand why you have to do that."

"If you knew the whole story…" He shakes his head and stands up, and I don't press him. I'm not going to. What I am going to do is find a hidden crying spot later so I can weep for the fourteen-year-old boy who became this man. Leo reaches down, takes my elbow, and lifts me to my feet. "Brush," he says. "Clothes." His voice drops back into his usual command. "Bed."

CHAPTER SEVENTEEN

Haley

LEO FINDS A hairbrush and works it through my hair. He dresses me in his own clothes, walks me to his bed, and puts me in. I'm ready to protest. Ready to insist that I'm not tired. Ready to provoke him, even. Anything to get more of this closeness. But the moment he pulls the covers up to my shoulders, my eyelids droop and I'm out. Sleep claims me.

I don't know if he ever comes to bed. I sleep all night. It's the sleep of a narrow miss. Of a near thing. My body dives in deep. Heat comes in waves over my cheeks any time I get close to resurfacing, but I can't pinpoint why.

In the morning I wake up alone.

There's a different kind of silence in Leo's bedroom. A more expansive one. The room itself is bigger than the guest room, but more importantly, Leo is gone. I know he's not here the instant I'm conscious. He always seems larger than life. Like he takes up so much space. Now I know that it's not him, or not only him. The pain he carries with him is a stack of barbed, humming energy. That takes up space, too.

I could sleep for longer. All day. All night.

But I get out of bed and go drowsily down the long, long hallway to the guest room. I notice two things right away. One, the bed is made. I didn't sleep here last night. I slept in Leo's bed. I slept in his bed.

Which could be related to the second thing that's different.

The phone on the bedside table.

My phone.

I tiptoe over to it until I catch myself being ridiculous and loom over the phone. It's…charging. Not plugged in, but charging. I pick it up and it stops. Put it back on the bedside table, and the screen lights up. The table of Leo's guest room has a built-in charger.

Wow.

I swipe my thumb over the screen, and the phone unlocks. This is really my phone, then. He gave it back. I feel like the human embodiment of a warm, sparkling glow, which is crazy. People don't glow for Leo Morelli. They run from him, or hurt for him, or—

Or touch him like they want to.

No more thoughts. Only phone calls.

Cash answers on the first ring. "Jesus, Hales." His voice is pinched. My heart sinks right through Leo's plush carpeting. "Did they tell you?"

"Tell me what?" I pace around the bed and back. "Cash, did something happen?"

A door shuts in the background of his call. "Aunt Caroline happened. She's trying to have Dad committed."

I sit down heavily on the side of the mattress. "What do you mean, committed?"

I know what he means, but only in the vague, horrified sense that it can't be right. It cannot be right. My dad is too trusting, and he spends too much time working, but that doesn't mean Caroline can have him put away.

"There's a hospital upstate." Despite the obvious strain, Cash keeps his tone level. That's how I know it's bad. "An old-fashioned asylum type of place, where they keep people."

I'm half off the bed. Maybe it's to throw up. Maybe it's to run. I'll run all the way home if I have to. "Tell me he's not there already. Tell me she didn't take him."

"She didn't take him yet."

That's the thing about Caroline Constantine.

She could come to my house and take my father. Would she do it personally, with her own two hands? No. She would not. That's not the Constantine way. The Constantine way is to hire out the dirtiest work so your hands always stay clean. The memory of Leo's shadowed form pinning that man to the alley wall drills through me. Leo killed those men with his own two hands. With his own knife. He's a Morelli. He's not supposed to have more integrity than even the worst Constantines.

And yet.

I push myself off the bed and go to the window. With my forehead pressed against the glass, I do deep breathing and focus on the snowflakes swirling down over Leo's beautiful backyard. No—grounds. He has grounds. Caroline has her claws in my dad. I have a shirt that belongs to Leo, and a pair of too-big pajama pants more luxurious than anything in my closet back home.

"He's in the house, Cash? Dad's home?"

"He's home for now. I don't want him to hear—" Cash clears his throat and lowers his voice. "Caroline's bulldog came to visit. That guy, Ronan. He threatened him. Pushed him around in his workshop. Broke some shit." A pause that sounds like a struggle.

A guilty ache closes in around my neck, holding on so tight I can't catch my breath. "Cash," I try. "I—"

I don't know what to do. I'm here with Leo, and Cash is in the most dangerous place on earth. Caroline Constantine owns Bishop's Landing and most of the people in it. If she brought enough of them to our house, they would have all the power.

This is what it must be like to be crumpled up and thrown away. I feel folded in. Caved. Discarded, though I came here on my own.

If Aunt Caroline takes our dad away, then all of this will have been for nothing. I took the strap for Leo. Took his cock down my throat. Bandaged his wounds. It will all be meaningless.

Part of me shrinks away from that thought, disgusted. Those things we did—they meant something. But Leo and I signed a deal, and emotions weren't part of it. It's confusing. I don't know which way is up.

"Are you okay, Hales?"

"Yes," I squeak, then clap my hand over my mouth to keep in the sobs. I've gotten better at keeping them silent while I'm here. It comes in handy right now. I have to let this out some way or another, but it's not going to be in front of my brother. "I'm going to be fine. What's our plan?"

I wish Petra was here to swoop in and arrange things with drill-sergeant precision. You never had to worry about finding your place when your sister was in charge. She had the answers to every question. Her word was law.

There's only one person I know—other than Petra—who always has an answer.

That person is Leo Morelli.

The flush that spreads from my neck down makes me back away from the window. I cannot fantasize about a mortal enemy of our family when he's the reason Aunt Caroline is after my dad in the first place.

That obnoxious, relentless voice in my head spins up. Leo Morelli didn't start this.

No. Of course he didn't. The feud between the Morellis and the Constantines started long before Leo came to my dad with his contract. Leo is making moves in a game that's older than both of us.

"Hales?" Cash's voice sounds far away, but my thoughts are too frantic, too loud. Aunt Caroline is the one who's had a problem all these years. Aunt Caroline is the one who wanted my dad to be different. Leo chose him because Aunt Caroline has always kept him on the outside. She wouldn't help him, and that left us vulnerable to

Leo. I can't untangle what it means. I can't find the thread that gets us out of this.

Leo was supposed to be the threat. Not Aunt Caroline.

"I'll come home. We'll figure it out. It'll be better if I—"

"No." Cash's voice is so decisive that it shocks me into silence. "I'm handling it. You have to stay there, with him."

There's such venom in his voice that it seeps through the phone. "Cash, there has to be something—"

"Stay where you are." He's forcing the words through gritted teeth. Cash is never this angry. Never at the mercy of his emotions like this. Of the two of us, he's the real Constantine. Cool under pressure. Delightful at parties. He doesn't get pissed and speak to people like this. "Keep Leo Morelli away. That's all you have to do."

CHAPTER EIGHTEEN

Haley

I'M A MESS.

Keeping it together, at least outwardly, is the best and only option. I can't have a screaming, panicking meltdown. That's not me. And it won't get me anywhere. It definitely won't get Aunt Caroline to leave my dad alone. It won't help Cash. We'll still be in trouble.

If it was summer, I would go for a run to clear my head. I would run until the pattern of my footfalls put everything back in order again. But it's winter. I'm certain Leo has a gym here, but the logistics make me want to go back to bed. Calling Mrs. Page for clothes. Finding it. Running on a treadmill, which I'm certain is a preview of hell.

No.

Instead, I shower. Dry my hair. Smooth some product over it that makes it slightly sleeker. Slightly shinier. Stare at myself in the mirror while I try to get my brain to work.

A pink box waits for me when I step back into the room. More new clothes, these ones even softer than the previous outfit. I put on the underthings and black leggings and long-sleeved shirt and stare into the bottom of the box. There is no humiliating lingerie. Not a scrap of it.

I don't know what it says about me that I'm slightly disappointed.

No Mrs. Page in the hallway. No Gerard. The dining room downstairs is empty. I wonder if Leo's out on business. He must be. He can't be staying here all day, every day, just because we have an agreement.

I don't long for him. God, no. Not at all. I just rub my knuckles against my chest and walk the halls until I find myself in his den. The built-in bookshelves pull me in like a current in deep water. There. Yes. It feels better with my hands on the spines of books. I pull one down at random and flip it open.

It's Leo's.

The neat print of his name inside the front cover makes me look twice to confirm that it is in fact his name inside a book. A book he intends to keep, since I can't imagine he sends anything with his name on it to used book sales. Not like my family. Our house churns with books. They come in, they go out, they get sold back to the student bookstore. There isn't space to keep all the books I've loved, anyway. The only other mansions I've visited, like Aunt Caroline's, have shelves full of decorative fakes and a few uncut first editions for looks.

This is the real thing. There's even a crease in the spine.

I fold it to my chest like a life preserver and take it to the armchair closest to the fireplace. It's classic sci-fi. I fall headfirst into it like a swooning teenager, which is embarrassing, because I know in my heart that it's not the plot or the characters or even the perfectly fine writing that's doing it for me.

It's Leo's name inside the cover.

Chapters tick by, page by page by page, the light outside the windows shifting from one winter glow to the next. Dusk comes, and so does Mrs. Page. She turns on a low lamp nearby without asking and replaces my tea. Not long after I trade my prim seated position for a slouch and then finally let my legs dangle over the arm of the chair.

That's how I'm sitting when I feel the presence in the doorway.

Leo leans against the doorframe, watching me with undisguised amusement. He's dressed for the office in what's obviously a custom suit, judging by how well it fits him. "You've made yourself at home."

I swing my legs forward and tug at my clothes. "I *am* home, according to our contract."

He laughs, and I expect him to say something cutting about how a Constantine could never be at home here. But he doesn't. His eyes sweep over the room. I follow his gaze. The evidence of my daylong staycation in his den is on the side table. My last mug of tea. A plate with a half-eaten sandwich. A can of Diet Coke I haven't opened.

"Mrs. Page says you've spent all day here."

"It's a decent book."

"Not the best book?" It's not fair how good he looks in the suit. And under the suit.

"The best book is Jane Eyre, obviously." Nobody can argue that point with me.

"Yet you've spent an entire day of your life sitting in my den reading something mediocre. You love reading enough to settle?"

"No. Leather furniture turns me on."

Surprise bursts across Leo's face like a sunbeam through clouds. It's gone almost instantly, fitted back into his usual piercing expression. He straightens up. "Get up and get dressed."

I'm on my feet embarrassingly quickly. "I'm already dressed."

"Not for going out, you're not. Mrs. Page." She's there instantly, like he snapped his fingers and made her appear from thin air. "Haley needs a dress. We'll leave in twenty minutes."

What am I supposed to do, question it? I don't. Of course I don't. I climb the stairs to the guest bedroom and make myself slightly more presentable. My hair is flat on one side from all the reading, so I fix that. There's makeup in neutral colors in one of the guest bathroom drawers, everything new and in the package. Leo's sister has thought of absolutely everything. The only thing she couldn't do was match foundations in advance. She solved that problem by putting ten of them in the drawer, all miniatures. By the time Mrs. Page bustles in with a garment bag I look pink-cheeked and human.

Part of me dreads this. Going out was never supposed to be part of this arrangement. Going out is for people who are in real relationships, or at least dating each other. At the same time, I'm...excited? Yes. It's excitement that makes my heart beat this way.

Last night rattled my brain. He saved me, and

he let me in, and there's nothing I want more.

Mrs. Page unzips the garment bag and pulls out a gown. It's a gorgeous champagne gold. I would never have picked this out for myself. The color wouldn't look good with my pale complexion, would it? I hold it up to the mirror. It looks…effervescent. Shimmering. I seem otherworldly in this color. "You've got four minutes left." She's brought underthings and shoes, too—the kind that go with a gown like this. Delicate and expensive in a matching gold color. "Step in, quick as you can. Mr. Morelli doesn't like to be kept waiting."

I abandon all previous shyness and focus on dressing. "Do you know where he's taking me?"

"Somewhere in the city, I would think. He didn't give me any specifics."

"Maybe next time," I say wistfully, but secretly I like this, too.

With one minute to spare, I go down to meet Leo at the front doors. He watches me come down the stairs with a light in his eyes that I'm sure I imagine. Leo offers me his arm when I reach him, and I swallow a giggle.

I am not going to giggle in front of him. Jesus Christ.

Leo's driver is waiting for us by the black SUV

in the circle drive. He opens the door for us and jogs around to the front. We get in and go.

"Are you going to tell me where we're going?" I ask when we're closer to the city.

Leo gives me an indulgent smile. "It's a surprise."

I make a face. Having a creative inventor for a father has given me a dislike for surprises. There are only so many times you can wake up with freezing water flooding the second floor of your house before it stops being exciting. "Just tell me."

He gives a low chuckle. His face isn't visible in the shadows of the limo, but I can imagine his expression—subtly amused, darkly challenging. "You can guess."

"A restaurant."

"No."

"A movie?"

The faint sound of a scoff. "You know me better than that, Haley."

Do I? It's an intriguing idea, that I might know Leo Morelli. He seems unknowable. A mystery. No one could have him figured out, but he seems to think I might. "A charity gala."

"No, darling. That's much too tame for what I have in mind tonight."

I'm left to imagine the possibilities. We

wouldn't go dancing, would we? I've heard that Leo likes to visit clubs, but maybe he doesn't— maybe he only uses them, the way he uses everything else. As a distraction and a shield. Maybe it *is* a restaurant and he's just keeping me on my toes by saying no. I spend the last few minutes of the drive swinging between nerves and delight at the thought of eating with him in public. It would be a relief, honestly. Being a not-rich Constantine means that meals out are rare and come with a side of pressure to do the right thing, to not spend too much, to not eat too little.

Leo would order for me, probably. And there would never be any question about the cost.

But we don't pull up in front of a restaurant.

The driver guides the SUV into an alley behind a sprawling building. I get goose bumps. The urge to run tenses all the muscles in my legs. But Leo wouldn't do that. He wouldn't take me to some random alley just to fuck with me.

"I had a separate team come ahead of us," Leo mentions, scrolling through a screen on his phone. He taps at something there. "They cleared out the four blocks surrounding this building. There's no one in the alley."

"I wasn't worried about it."

Bullshit, his expression says. But he only waits

for the driver to open the door and helps me step out.

We're directly in front of a short flight of stairs leading to a wide doorway. There's a panel set into the wall next to the frame. Leo punches in a code, something clicks in the door, and I'm gripped with the fear that I'm about to witness something worse than the revenge killing of three men in an alley. For all I know, the rest of Leo's family could be waiting behind this door.

I'm wrong again. The only person waiting on the other side is a uniformed guard who is not at all surprised to see us. "Mr. Morelli." He smiles like Leo is a friend. "You picked a good night. Last night we had visitors."

"Visitors?" Leo's skeptical. "Who the hell did you let in here? I should have you fired."

The guard laughs, and I feel like I'm in some other universe. Some other plane of existence where Leo Morelli is not a universal monster. "Rich guy. Had too much money, like you, and a wife who cried."

"Who cries at a library?"

I shake myself loose from the shock long enough to read a bronze sign on the wall. The New York Public Library. It's well after hours.

A wondering smile lights up the guard's face.

It's clear he saw something special. "This lady did, and then she laughed. Never seen anyone so excited to see all the books. And her man she came with—" He shakes his head. "Never seen anyone look at a woman quite like that."

"Like what?" Leo and the guard both glance at me, and my cheeks flush. "How did he look at her?"

The guard looks thoughtful, but Leo's watching me. "Like he'd have stopped his own heart if it would make her happy. He'd have gone that far. It wouldn't have made her happy, though. She was like a little moon. Constantly near him. Constantly holding his hand. You should have seen how many people he sent to clear the building beforehand. Didn't matter. That man didn't let her out of his sight for a second." A blink. "He had weird eyes, that guy. Never asked him about it. He wasn't the chatty type. Not like you."

Leo claps the guy on the shoulder. "You call me if he comes back."

"Why? Does he sound like your type?"

"No. I want to tell him to fuck off out of my library." A joke, from Leo to the guard.

"I'll give you a call. But don't let me get in your way." He steps back to let us pass by. "You know where you're going?"

"I think I *will* have you fired, just for that insult. This way, Haley." He puts a big hand on the small of my back and warmth spreads out from my spine to the tips of my fingers.

It takes a minute before I can speak. We're waiting at an elevator, both of us watching the numbers tick down. "You have tons of books in your house already."

"Not this book."

The elevator takes us to the third floor. Down the hall we enter a rotunda that reminds me of Leo's house as much as anything. An arched ceiling. Intricate murals on the walls. Miles and miles of dark paneling. My heels feel mortifyingly loud in what's basically a cathedral. We pass through another room with soaring windows, low desks, and catalogs, and then I feel ridiculous because the rotunda wasn't the cathedral.

The reading room is.

Leo takes me inside like he's been here every day of his life. Maybe he has. A full-body shiver moves through me. It's a massive room, with long tables and a ceiling that belongs inside a palace. Silence like this is rare in New York City. Rare in places where people crowd together. I desperately want to sit at one of those tables, surrounded by books and whispers, but standing here with Leo is its own out-of-body experience.

"You've never been here." He's watching me, I realize, and I look like I just got off the bus from the middle of nowhere America.

"There wasn't a lot of time." I always meant to go, and things came up. My dad would get on Caroline's bad side again, or something would go wrong in his workshop, or Cash would need someone at financial aid meetings. A thousand reasons. And one that I'll never mention, which is that I never felt worthy of visiting places like this in the city.

Leo sighs. "I should fuck you on one of these tables. The sounds would be magnificent." He gazes up at the ceiling. "Let's go."

His words have me hot, on the verge of squirming. "Go where?"

"I didn't bring you here to bend you over a table in the reading room."

I can't breathe. For all the things we've done, and all the things he's done to me, he still hasn't taken me. My heart feels oversized. It's squeezing out all the room in my lungs. This can't be real, and I can't want it this much, and I absolutely cannot be on a date with Leo Morelli.

"I think that's allowed under the contract," I

murmur. I want to sound sophisticated, as if I wouldn't mind either way. Instead it comes out breathy. Needy.

His hand is instantly around my neck, instantly making it that much harder to breathe, and I arch in his grip. Leo laughs, and he's right—every sound is amplified here, made magic. He leans down and presses a kiss to the side of my neck, above his fingers. "I would love to break open that pretty little pussy right now." His hand flexes, and it's with obvious effort that he traces his fingers down my neck and over my collarbone. "But there's something I want to show you first."

I feel like human champagne. Leo moves his hand to the back of my neck, which is somehow both hotter and more demeaning, and rubs a thumb up and down while he walks me down the long aisle to another room.

This one is dark too, except for one light on a table in the center of the room. The glow falls away into shadow but I can see the double-decker shelves with stairs, the polished wood, the books...

A dream. All this is a dream come true, including, impossibly, the man in his perfect suit, striding toward that table with its lamp. He turns to watch me walk toward him and I do it through the unreality of this moment. A midnight library. Leo, with dark heat in his eyes. And a book, waiting for me on the table.

I come to the edge of the light and look. "You're kidding."

"I'm not."

"This is a first edition." I lean in closer, afraid to breathe. "Is this real?"

"No. I had a fake first edition of Jane Eyre manufactured and planted in the New York Public Library just to fuck with you."

"You would do something like that." Every inch of me thrums with tense excitement. The book seems real enough. I've seen photos of other rare copies like this, and it looks right. If it is, this book—this one single book—is worth more than sixty thousand dollars. It could pay for all my student loans. "You're—"

"The Beast of Bishop's Landing, yes." I feel, rather than see, Leo rolling his eyes. "That doesn't alter the reality of this book." It's propped up on a stand meant to make it easy to open the pages. I bite my lip and reach out to open the front cover. Leo grabs my wrist with a second to spare. It's an electric, possessive touch, and that lightning is reflected in his eyes. "Hold out your hands first."

I do it. They're shaking. He takes a plastic

bottle from his pocket, pulls us away from the table, and sprays my hands. Then he follows it up with an actual cloth handkerchief that feels more expensive than his shirts or sheets. Leo dries every one of my fingers individually. "As clean as you'll get," he pronounces, and then he lets me go back to the book.

The first page confirms that it's not, in fact, a trick.

Jane Eyre, it reads.
An Autobiography.
Edited by Currer Bell.

There's more, but tears in my eyes make it hard to see. This is my favorite book. My *favorite.*

"A Constantine crying over a book." Leo's words have no bite. "Why?"

"I love this book." It feels overwhelming, the love I have for this book. Or maybe it's the moment. The pool of light in a dark room. The man at the edge of that light. "The whole story. The nanny, and Mr. Rochester, and his crazy wife in the attic. It's—" I'm getting choked up. "It's romantic. I miss it when I'm not reading it."

The corner of his mouth turns up. "You think *he* is romantic. And he keeps his wife in the attic."

"He has a secret that hurts him, and he tries to

keep it from hurting Jane for as long as he can. And he gave it all up for her in the end. He was waiting for her. Mourning."

That's romantic, I'm going to say, but I can't say anymore. I can't explain it, or the rush of feeling and ache and empathy. Can't begin to explain it. Before I can try, before I can open my mouth, Leo's fingers are on my jawline. He turns my head. I get one glimpse of his eyes, those gold-shot wells of old pain and lust, and then he kisses me. It's hot and hard and confident. The way I imagine Mr. Rochester would be when Jane returned to him.

CHAPTER NINETEEN

Haley

LEO PICKS ME up as easily as I'd pick up a book, but I can't care about anything but the feel of his mouth on mine. His tongue is skilled and searing and the deepest, most hidden part of me sighs with relief. God, it's so good. It's so right, and so forbidden. Villains aren't supposed to kiss the virtue out of you. Did I ever have any to begin with?

He sets me on a table and knocks my legs apart so he can stand between them, forcing them to stay that way with his body while he drags his mouth down the side of my neck. Nipping. Biting. Every movement makes my core clench tight, then tighter, curling around a burst of embarrassment that I've never been kissed this way before. No one has ever come close. Compared to Leo, every man I've ever known is a worthless, fumbling boy.

I'm on top of books. Open books.

Leo twists his fingers into my hair and tips my head back so he can lick sensitive skin and I have to steady myself with one hand. It meets pages. There is a project out on this table, someone's work or someone's story, and Leo doesn't care. He ordered them out. He made them bring the book for me. Sixty-thousand-dollar books don't sit out in rooms like this. He made this happen.

He's hard between my legs when he breaks the kiss. For a long moment he stares above my head, catching his breath with both hands wrapped around the sides of my face. His eyes—Jesus. His eyes. It's the way he looked at me when he told me he wasn't hurt. All of his pain and lust and need are there at the surface, in plain sight. This time there's no lie on his lips.

I reach for him, and he doesn't stop me.

He lets me run my fingers down the line of his jaw. He lets me skim the shoulder of his jacket. He lets me brush my fingertips over his lips, his eyes glittering and black. I move to pull my fingers away, but Leo catches the tips between his teeth and bites. It pulls a stifled moan out of me, that sharp, pointed pain. He bites harder, teeth digging into flesh, but then he sucks my fingers into his mouth and soothes the marks. I don't know how he does it, creating a direct line from my fingertips to my clit, but he does.

Leo turns me over with a low laugh that's familiar and scary and hot. He presses me facedown into the books and shoves my dress up over my hips. "Oh, no," I hear myself say. "Oh, no."

But nothing is wrong except how filthy he's being. He puts a knee between my thighs and spreads me open with big hands. And then Leo Morelli licks me over the lace of the lingerie. The slick heat of his tongue through cloth is so new it makes my knees buckle. Leo won't let me fall. He only licks higher, to a far more forbidden spot, and drills his tongue into it. The delicate twists of lace and wet heat have me panting, embarrassed. He licks me again, again, again, and when he takes his tongue away, a tear runs down my cheek.

"Fuck, I love that," he says from somewhere above me. "A pretty thing like you, crying for more."

It's true. I am. I shouldn't want this, shouldn't want any part of being fucked over a table by my family's enemy, but I've never wanted anything more.

Leo tears the panties away. The lace doesn't go without a fight. It burns on its last trip across my skin. Cool air reaches between my legs, lighting up every wet part of me, made wetter because he wanted it. It's too hot to bear. I squirm into the table, rocking my hips mindlessly. Leo slaps his palm over my pussy and I jolt, the startle descending into more shivers.

"I was wrong about you. I thought I'd tease you with candlelight and gentle hands, but that's not what you need." He tests my thighs, then slides his thumbs up higher and higher and higher until he uses them to spread my ass, wider than before. I'd be frozen if it weren't for the trembling. Exposed like this, bent over in this enormous room, air caressing parts of me that no one has ever seen except the woman who waxes me. One of the only things I'll let myself waste money on, and god, I'm glad for it now. "Hold yourself open for me. I'm going to make you cry harder."

It's awkward as hell, reaching back the way he wants me to, and harder than I would ever have imagined. If I had ever imagined doing this. Once my hands are in place and my nipples are crushed against the pages underneath me, Leo settles himself back between my legs and resumes his own project.

His tongue on bare skin is too much. My hips buck against the table hard enough to bruise. I still can't stop. Not until he puts his tongue in that place again. "No, no, no," I chant.

"You gave this to me, too. Did you forget?" A sharp slap on the side of my ass, then another five. "Don't let your hands slip. My belt works as well as a strap."

My hips move involuntarily, remembering that strap. Is this what people mean when they say *delirious*? My vision's blurred, but I'll be damned if I don't follow his orders.

If I let go, he'll hurt me. *Do it*, a voice whispers in the back of my mind. *Let go. Let him hurt you. He does it so well.* That's the awful, depraved truth. He does it so well, and it makes me so wet, and I know he would make me come after. He would.

Thick fingers press against my asshole, and my breath stops. No one. Never. Not until Leo.

"Fuck, you're tight here. This won't be easy, darling. Take a breath."

I'm halfway through that breath when he sinks those fingers into me up to the knuckle. Oh, fuck. Oh, Jesus. His fingers are huge. They stretch me, they burn, and he's not stopping. My head comes up off the books, which makes me tense and tighten, and Leo pushes it down with his free hand.

He forces his fingers farther in. My gasp echoes off the ceiling. "That's it," he croons. "Fight me. Don't for a second relax that tight hole and let me in."

The second he says it, I can't resist him. I stop trying to lift my head and focus all my energy on relaxing. It doesn't seem possible until it happens. Leo pushes his fingers the rest of the way in with a hiss. "Good girl." His laugh spills over me like red wine. "That was hot, the way you clenched when I said that. You get another finger."

"Too much," I beg, even while I dig my fingers into my own flesh to keep myself exposed for him. "I can't take it."

"Cry if you need to."

I do need to. The stretch and burn intensifies until tears leak down onto book pages, until my cunt is nothing but a wet ache. This is the meanest thing that anyone's ever done to me. I never want it to stop. I can't catch my breath when his fingers are seated. Leo doesn't care. He reaches between my legs with his other hand and pinches my clit. I don't recognize the sound that comes out of me. A plaintive whine. A begging cry. Leo makes a noise in the back of his throat that makes me tighten on his fingers again.

"You're not going to come tonight unless it's

on my fingers." His voice is low and rough in my ear. "Or on my cock. Fingers first, I think."

He strokes between my legs and my face is hot enough to catch the books on fire. To curl the pages and send them up in smoke. I can't stop the tears. I don't know if they're from wanting to come more than I want to breathe, or how much my asshole hurts stretched around his fingers, or from the horrifying truth that I like this. I need this. My orgasm has been waiting, struggling against the pain, but under his expert fingers it winds up and snaps.

Coming on his fingers is a thousand times more intense when those fingers are stretching a virgin hole. He keeps them in deep while I ride it out. They seem even bigger by the end. Too big. So big. I only discover I'm saying this out loud when Leo answers.

"Yes. You're fucking tiny, and tight. Your pussy will stretch too, darling. It won't have any choice."

He turns me over onto my back and fresh heat flares on my face. I'm tearstained and panting and disheveled. The pretty gown he dressed me in is up around my waist. This is as intimate as when he told me his secrets. He's the secret now. He's going to be the mark on my skin that never goes away. Leo puts one hand on the inside of each of my thighs and spreads my legs again. I have one hand curled around the spine of a book and the other gripping a handful of pages. I'm trying to be careful. I might hurt them, too.

"Christ, you're sweet." This, he says so softly that I'm not sure he means to say it to me. I was expecting a fast, hard fuck, but Leo leans down and kisses my clit, swirling his tongue over it until I come. He shifts positions to lick me while the pleasure rolls over. I can't hear him over the pounding of my heart, but I can feel the vibrations of his voice on my pussy. Like I'm the best thing he's ever tasted. Like this one thing lets the world hurt less.

He straightens up when my orgasm is finished and wipes his mouth on his sleeve, his eyes hard on mine. "I'm going to fuck you now. Make you bleed. It's going to hurt, and I'm going to love that. It's going to sting, and ache, and stretch. You're going to cry. I'm going to love that, too. And I promise you, darling, I won't take my cock away and stop hurting you until you come." A pause that seems weighted with meaning and the harsh pull of my breath. "That's the deal."

If I weren't already lying down, I'd fall. I'd swoon right to the ground. Because even with his hands on my thighs, even with his body barring me from closing my legs, Leo is asking permission.

It's permission he doesn't need.

He could have taken me the night I stepped foot in his house. He has my name on a contract. He owns me, and he owns my family, and this dark-suited devil is giving me an out.

"Please." My dry mouth doesn't help. "Please hurt me."

A curt nod. He's coiled tight, too. I see it now in the set of his shoulders and the tension in his jaw. Leo's hands make fast work of his belt.

His cock has been down my throat, but I'm shocked at the sight of it. How thick and wanting it is. A bead of precum catches the lamplight. I never thought I'd be in the position of admitting that a Morelli is perfect, but there's no other word for him. Beautiful and terrifying and perfect.

He drags his crown through my folds, getting it slick. At the pressure against my opening, I want to close my eyes. But I can't look away.

Leo braces his hands on my hips, stroking me with the full width of his palms, and I don't fully process how much it calms me until he makes the first thrust.

My scream bounces back at both of us, off the

ceiling, and Leo curses under his breath.

I can't move. He's so big. I can't—I can't do anything. He's splitting me in two. My mind struggles with it, tries to make the pain into pleasure, but it's like speaking a foreign language. I don't know pain the way he does. Pages crumple in my fist. Leo works his way in another inch, his whole body fighting him. I can tell how much he wants to fuck me. It's obvious, it's obvious. Tears leak from the corners of my eyes. He sweeps one of them away with the pad of his thumb.

His cock pulses inside me, and his chest heaves with big breaths. He was not lying when he said he would love my tears and my pain. He *does* love it. But it's not simple, no, no, no. It's not simple at all. He wrestles with it. I can see that struggle in his eyes.

With another curse, Leo gathers me up in strong arms, keeping himself inside me. There's a rug on the floor, an oval of light on it, and he takes us there. Lowers us to the floor. I'm on top of him now. Being on top gives me no more control. He puts one hand on the floor to steady him and uses the other to arrange me. My knees touch the floor, but barely, my thighs aching with the effort of keeping myself hovering above his thick cock.

"I can't take anymore," I sob. "It won't fit."

He makes a shushing sound, his face a picture of need. Leo lifts one hand to brush my hair away from my cheek. "I always keep my promises, and now you're going to help me. Be a good girl."

The edge in his voice is a ploy. It's mean, but I want it. And underneath is something else. I didn't think Morellis were capable of feeling empathy, but he is.

Not that that's going to stop him from doing this.

Not that it's going to stop me.

Leo leans up and nips the side of my jaw, then presses kisses on the mark. "Bleed for me, darling. Give it to me."

"It hurts." More tears. So many they roll down to his jacket like rain. He moves to unbutton it. Black jacket, black shirt. I slide my hands under the lapels and hold on tight. Gravity pulls me down another inch. "You're too big."

He presses a knuckle to my clit and rubs it in a slow, teasing circle. Another clench, another wash of wetness. "But your pussy likes it."

I drop my head forward, grip his shirt for dear life, and concentrate on the rhythmic roll over my clit. Another inch. Another. Sweat beads on my hairline. He's remaking me with his cock. I'm going to be a new person at the end of this. Trial by fucking. The circles continue until shadows crowd in at the edges of my vision and another orgasm tackles me forcefully from behind. I sob through the whole thing. I can't stop impaling myself on his cock, can't get the orgasm to let me go, and can't push past the last place inside me holding him back. "Help me. Please. *Please.*"

Leo's cock throbs inside me and he sits up, his muscles bunching. He wraps one hand around the back of my head and presses my face into his shoulder. "Bite." I get a mouthful of his jacket. Then his hands are on my hips. "Big breath." It's a noisy, embarrassing breath, sucked in through his clothes. "Ready?"

I nod feverishly, desperate for him to do this, desperate to be on the other side of this, desperate to be closer to him.

He meets that desperation with a vicious stroke, using his hands to drive me down harder, to take my virginity with more force.

My scream starts out anguished, unrecognizable. But when he's all the way inside, when he's taken every inch of me... Heat. A deep-down heat, a fiery one. I feel it everywhere he is, and it trips through my veins like I'd imagine drugs would. I'm sobbing but the sobs turn into moans.

Leo puts his hand back behind him. Oh—*oh*. It's because I'm fucking him for real now. His eyes are half-closed, teeth gritted, and it's been hard for him to wait. He held back for so long.

Now he ruts into me like the beast he is, forceful and feral. It is absolutely not possible for me to come again, but pleasure hitches itself to the pain of being fucked for the first time. It takes me by the hips. It grinds me down onto Leo's cock and makes me dance for it. "Good," I hear myself say. "Good, please. Good."

What are you waiting for? I think the question, because I can't form real sentences.

He doesn't answer with words. He only waits, his eyes dark embers.

A final, ragged orgasm wraps me up and shakes itself through my whole body. Leo comes when I'm at the peak, cock jerking. It's hot, hot, hot inside. There must be so much cum. He makes a low, animal sound. I could listen to him do that every day. It carves out a new craving at the heart of me.

He puts a hand on my face and keeps watch, eyes on mine, all the way to the bitter end.

CHAPTER TWENTY

Leo

I WANT TO keep Haley here forever.

I never want to coax her off my shoulder. I never want to leave this room. I never want the sun to rise.

She's panting, one hand fisted in my shirt, a long time later. I run a hand over her hair. "We can't stay all night."

Haley stirs, sighing. "I thought Morellis could do anything they wanted."

"It would be amusing to keep fucking you until the first patrons arrive. You're right." Her breathing picks up. She would find a little public play hot. There are places for that, but I I won't let it happen. Let other people see her sweet cunt? No. Fuck no. "However, I have other ideas."

"Like a bath in your bathtub?"

More along the lines of tying her to the bed and fucking her ass, just so I can say I've taken her in every hole. I want her so powerfully that I could do it right now. Sadly, there's a limit to how much a thing like Haley could take before I'd have to carry her out of here. The guard can be bribed, of course, but if I destroy her the way I want to...

Well. People would talk.

"Like a bath." This convinces her to lift her head. I have to help her to her feet and rearrange the dress. I use my handkerchief to dab between her legs, which makes her hiss. I find her ruined panties and shove them into my pocket, then make a halfhearted attempt at smoothing out the pages of the books on the table. Casualties of a good fuck. There are worse ways to die. "One last look at your favorite thing."

Haley's blue eyes are huge, and they linger on me for so long that my skin tingles.

"The book," I prompt.

She blinks. "Right. Yes." Haley goes back to the table and bows her head over it, reverent, and uses her pinky finger to close the front cover. "Goodbye," she whispers. "You're beautiful."

My chest seizes up. As soon as she's asleep, I'm getting people out of bed. This book is going to be mine, and then it's going to be hers. This copy of Jane Eyre is technically a witness to her very first real fuck. It can't be left to the world.

Haley comes back to me on unsteady legs and takes my hand.

It's a near miss. I almost let it show, how good it feels, and that's too far. We're already outside the bounds of the rest of my life. I'll let my sisters hug me, if that's what they need to do, but holding hands with a woman—

It's not a good decision, if history is any indication. Still, I don't think anything short of a bomb dropped on this building would inspire me to let go. Maybe not even that.

It's a measured walk back through the main reading room. Haley tries her best to move quietly, and the mood is hushed, almost reverent. What happened in that room, in full view of a first-edition Jane Eyre, was a sacrament. It moves with me now. Stays close, like the pain that dogs me every day of my life.

This is different. I wouldn't describe it as an emotion. More like water to wine.

We take the elevator back down. Eugene, the guard, opens the door for us as we go. If he's been going between floors, if he heard anything, his face doesn't show it. On the way past him, I tuck several hundred-dollar bills into the pocket of his jacket. He pats them with his hand and pulls the door closed behind us.

It's a sharper, deeper cold, and I fold Haley into my side during the few steps to the SUV. Our coats, helpfully, wait for us in the backseat. I pull both of them over Haley's lap. My driver meets my eyes in the rearview mirror and shifts to drive.

She leans against me when we turn onto the street, and I can feel her hesitating. Like she thinks I might push her away.

I'm not going to push her away.

"Leo." There's hope in her voice. *Hope*. It's fucking terrifying, to hear that hope. It adds another layer of complexity to my revenge plot. The whole thing is getting out of hand.

My phone vibrates in my pocket before she can finish speaking.

I pull it out and frown at Trenton Alto's name. There's nothing planned for tonight, with him or with Lucian. Nothing business. Nothing social. I'm not interested in the street fights Trenton oversees. But in the interest of getting him to fuck off, I take the call.

"Don't waste my time," I say by way of greeting.

"Did you kidnap a Constantine?" Trenton laughs, and my gut goes cold. "It would be just like you to frame someone for a kidnapping."

"What the fuck are you talking about?"

"Lucian told me about your contract. He thinks it's funny as fuck. Some of your best work. But if you've gone beyond that, you should tell us so we can enjoy the show."

A surge of hatred at how often I make people sign contracts, at how ambiguous his statement is. It's highly unlikely that Trenton knows anything about Haley. My sisters and I have an unspoken agreement not to tell Lucian about things that go on in our houses, and Trenton hasn't been to my place in months. It's unlikely that he knows, but not impossible. "Who exactly did I kidnap?"

"The old man's gone missing. Settle our bet, Leo. Was it you or was it the Constantines who made him disappear?" Another laugh. "I don't know who'd be worse for that poor sap. If the Constantines found out about your contract, they'll put him down like a disloyal dog."

"I'll never tell." I hang up on him mid-laugh.

The blocks go by outside the window. I don't see any of them. This was what I wanted in the first place—to fuck with the tangled web of the Constantines. To keep them off-balance. To make them see each other as the threat to their sterling reputation. Above all, to bait a hook. This news should be a dream come true.

It feels like a nightmare.

Haley shifts against me, pulling away so she can see my face. "What's wrong?"

There's nothing I want to do less than look her in the eye, but I do it. I'm not a coward. I'm not going to lie to her. Hiding this development from her won't stop the sinking feeling in the pit of my gut. God, fuck. It was so good in that library. Fucking filthy, but pure, in a way.

Haley looks pleasantly tired. Well-fucked. Her cheeks are still pink. I can still feel her tight cunt gripping me. Lie to her. Every instinct sinks its claws into my skin. Lie. Lie. Lie.

"Your father's missing."

Her smile fades in increments, dropping away from the corners of her mouth first and falling until her lips—swollen from how hard I kissed her—are parted in horrified shock. Fat tears drop from her eyes. "He's not missing. I talked to my brother this morning. He wasn't missing this morning."

"He's missing now."

She licks her lips and raises her fingertips to touch them. The salt there seems to surprise her. Haley's tears are a reflex. An old one, I'd bet. The kind of reflex you can only have if your father loves you like a decent human instead of a

239

bloodthirsty fuck. "I talked to Cash this morning."

The partition between us and the driver has been up since we left my house to go to the library, so I tap out a text with her address and an order to stop at the next block. "Thomas is the driver. He's going to take you home."

Haley stares at me, uncomprehending, until the SUV slows and heads for the curb. "What's happening?" The note of panic in her voice flays me alive. "The thirty days—"

"Forget about the thirty days." I motion for Thomas to stay where he is and open the door.

She's crying harder now, trying to follow me out, and I have to block her in with my arm. "He's taking you home." Steady. Clear. I'd rather tear the SUV apart piece by piece than send her away in it, but this is where we are. "You need to look for your father."

"No."

"Yes." I take her face in my hands and kiss her forehead. It's ridiculously inadequate for this moment, but it has the effect I need—for Haley to stay in the car while I shut the door. When it clicks shut she tries for the handle. She's crying too hard to see it and misses her moment. Thomas is good at his job. He steers them back out into the road at the first opportunity.

Haley covers her eyes with her hands just before I lose sight of her.

It's a bitter night, and I don't have my coat. Fine. Good. My back is on fire. Maybe the frigid air will put it out soon. The answer right now is obviously to call Gerard and have him send a car, but I won't stand here like a jackass while I wait.

CHAPTER TWENTY-ONE

Haley

A CAR I don't recognize is parked in front of the garage. The driver, Thomas—who asked me more than once if I was all right—pulls in behind it and meets my eyes in the rearview mirror. "You okay to get out?"

"Yes. Thank you."

I'm not okay to get out. I'm half-hoarse from crying and my throat aches like I swallowed a knife. If I sit in this SUV one more second, I'm going to beg Thomas to drive me to Leo's house. I'd offer him anything to do it.

I can't let that become a habit.

The air outside is cold and dry and shocking, and it reminds me that I'm in an evening gown with only half a lingerie set underneath. A bizarre grief expands in my chest. Leo had other plans for tonight, and now I'll never know what they were. It doesn't matter. I run up the steps to the front door and shove it open. "Cash? Where are you?"

"I'm right here." He's sitting on the couch, back rigid, his jaw so tense I can hear his teeth grind together. "Hey, Hales."

"Cash, what—"

A man steps into view. He has dark hair and dark brows that dip low over intense eyes. His lips are a taut line. He looks scary when he's guarding my aunt, but it's nothing compared to now.

My stomach twists and drops. "Ronan." I can't just stop at saying his name. "Did Caroline send you? Where's my father?"

It's impossible not to notice the gun at his side. He's not trying to hide it. "He's here. She learned some unfortunate news about your father, and the family has decided it's best for him to stay home for the time being."

My father is a prisoner in his own home? My heart is trying its best to leap out of my body and follow my stomach to the pits of hell. "Is he working now? I'd like to see him."

"I'm not sure he's cooled down enough to talk."

Tiny hairs on the backs of my arms pull straight up. "My dad always wants to talk to me, even if he's busy. Where is he?"

Ronan gestures to the workshop door. It's closed. It's never closed. And there's something shiny and thick on the outside. A new lock. On the outside of the door.

They locked him in.

I take a deep, slow breath and try not to throw up.

"I'm going to go down and see my dad now." Cash stares straight ahead on the couch, not looking at me. One of his hands clenches into a fist and opens again. "You'll unlock the door."

Ronan considers this for so long I think he's going to tell me I can't go. I prepare myself to scream. To freak the fuck out. It's probably the most effective tool in my arsenal. Clearly, trading my body for my father's safety didn't work. A full-scale imitation of hysteria might.

"Fine," he says finally. "But if he causes any trouble, I'm locking you both in there."

Causes any trouble. Please. My father is distractible and too in love with his work, but that doesn't mean he's dangerous. The only trouble he causes is not being enough of a stuck-up asshole. I march over to the door and wait, arms folded over my chest, while Ronan undoes the lock. It's too much for the old wooden door. The sight of all that stainless steel makes me want to sink to my knees and cry.

I've done enough crying for now.

Ronan opens the door. Silence floats up the stairs, and a new fear pierces me. What if something happened to him while he was locked in? I take measured steps on the way down, like dignified walking is some kind of talisman. Three steps from the bottom, I get the courage to say something. "Daddy?"

A muffled noise. I leave the last step, and his workbenches come into full view. My dad is sitting next to one, shoulders hunched, his face in his hands. I rush across to him in my high heels. *Don't cry. Don't cry. Don't cry.*

"Daddy." I crouch down in front of him, and he uncovers his face. His skin is blotchy, eyes red. "Are you okay?"

"I wanted funding for my project. That's all." His voice quavers, and my heart breaks again. How many times can it do that before I die? "I didn't mean to do any harm. It's a good project."

A daughter should never see her father so desperate. "I know. I know." I take his hands in mine and begin the hopeless task of finding the right thing to say. "We'll figure it out."

"Caroline sent her man to lock me down here. He says I can't be trusted. *Me*. Untrustworthy. I've spent my life being trustworthy. All I've ever done is try to make things to help people. I can be trusted." His voice rises, and I'm acutely conscious of Ronan standing at the top of the stairs.

"You're right. You are. Aunt Caroline—" Ronan. Stairs. Close. "She sees things a different way. It's a misunderstanding. We'll smooth everything over."

"What about my invention?" He's so pale. So afraid. "It can't die with me."

"Daddy, you're not going to die. Nobody is going to let that happen. Let's let Caroline clear her head, and then we'll find a way to make things right with her." It makes me sick to think about appeasing her. "I'll make things right. You can concentrate on your work, and everything will go back to how it was."

Footsteps on the stairs. "Any trouble?" Ronan comes down into the workshop, and I hate him for it. I hate him so much.

"No trouble at all," I tell him.

"Except that I ruined everything." Dad's eyes darken. His blue eyes match mine, but his are clouded with tears and frustration. "I'm so sorry, honey. I never should have made that deal with Leo. I never should have let you go to him."

Ronan coughs behind me, covering up surprise. He didn't know. Leo kept his secret. He and his sisters didn't say a word about me to anyone. It's my own family putting me in danger. Aunt Caroline's hitman comes to stand closer. Of course he does. He wants to hear everything we say so he can take it back to his boss.

"You ruined things a little bit, yeah. But it'll be okay, Daddy. I'll fix everything."

My dad doesn't believe me. He drops his head, looking down at our hands. Ronan shouldn't be here for this moment. There's no need to humiliate my dad and make this harder than it has to be. I meet Ronan's eyes, ready to tell him to leave us alone, but his expression stops the words dead.

Pity is etched in his face.

Pity.

For me.

It should give me a sense of hope, that Caroline's man feels sympathy for us. But it scares me instead. Down to the bone. Down to the core of everything. Nothing but ice-coated fear, all the way down.

Ronan's pity is more terrifying than his gun. It's scarier than the violence he threatens just by being in the room. He's a man with no mercy. He would not hesitate to kill both of us. Pity on his face means there's a fate worse than death, if we don't fall in line.

I squeeze my dad's hand and let go, standing up before my knees protest the heels and the crouching. Ronan meets my eyes without flinching. He's more than fine with this job. "Will you be staying with us, then?"

"Until I'm called away."

Until we're dead, he means. Or until some more pressing assignment comes along. Please, let something more important come along. I take my dad's hand and pull him to standing with me. "Fine. When's the last time you had something to eat?"

"I don't remember." Dad shakes his head. "Earlier."

"Earlier today?"

"Could have been yesterday." He waves a hand in the air, then swallows hard. "It was easier to keep time when your mother was alive."

I meet Ronan's eyes and lift my chin. "I'm taking him to the kitchen."

Ronan has plenty of time to stop us. It's also plenty of time to feel how I don't fit in this house. I don't fit here in the dress. I don't fit here in this body. I don't fit here in spirit, either. My heart wants to be with Leo Morelli.

We walk together to the stairs, and Dad hesitates. He looks back over his shoulder at Ronan.

"Go ahead," he says. "I'll be right up."

CHAPTER TWENTY-TWO

Leo

I DON'T SLEEP.

I haunt the halls of my mansion like a ghost, snapping at Gerard and scowling at Mrs. Page from what seems like a great distance. Some of my people are looking for Haley's father. No word yet on whether they've found him. I shower in the gym, because I can't bring myself to go back to my own bedroom. On a day like today even water on the scars is like acid.

Sometime toward afternoon I end up in my office. The den is impossible. Sleep is impossible. Thank god for pain, my constant companion. I'll never be truly alone.

I'm not sure how long I've been glaring into space when Gerard comes in with soft footfalls and a very careful expression. "There's a visitor here to see you."

I have a moment of ecstatic, wild hope that it's Haley. "No need to draw this out. Tell me who the fuck it is."

"It's Caroline Constantine, sir."

A part of me blanches. That part is buried so deep that it won't ever rise to the surface. No one will ever know how the sound of her name makes me ill. I no longer react to it. I will never react to it again. "Send her in."

Gerard hesitates. "Are you sure?"

"Did I say to send her in or did I tell you to second-guess me like a man who's begging to be blacklisted and hunted down for sport?"

He nods and leaves.

I wait.

I don't wait long.

Caroline Constantine is dressed for the cold. All white. She looks like a twisted version of Haley. There's no sweetness to her. No kindness. Only a cultivated beauty from years of subtle plastic surgery and an anti-aging regimen that probably involves worshipping Satan. She strides into my office on stilettos, disapproval in her eyes. "Leo. No need to belabor the discussion."

As if we've been having a fucking discussion. "Hello, Caroline. It's so lovely to see you."

The words taste like ashes and lies.

"Yes, hello. I've come to dissolve the contract you've coerced my brother-in-law into signing."

I sit back in my seat and put on an air of mild confusion. "Coerced? He was perfectly willing. You have my word."

"I'm not sure your word is sufficient."

"I'm not sure you care about consent."

She frowns, her eyes flicking upward in a mimicry of a roll. "Don't be difficult. You and I both know your contract is exploitative, and I want it dissolved." Her tone grinds into my bones like pitted concrete. There was a time in my life when a hint of her haughty disapproval would have me scrambling to please her. Caroline lifts a hand and gestures vaguely in my direction. "I don't find this attitude attractive."

Disgusting.

Caroline is disgusting, and my entire soul recoils from her. It recoils from the barrage of memories. Every one is an old assault made into a new one. She seemed invincible when I was younger. Untouchable. So when she let me touch her, I thought it was worth something. I was so fucking naive. And I was an easy target. She was willing to give the illusion of approval, and I wanted it so much I was willing to debase myself for it.

That's no longer the case.

Caroline is drawn up to her full height on the

other side of the desk, as if being on her feet gives her an advantage. I let the silence stretch out. She's the one who taught me about silence. About its power. About the way it invites shame. Silence will spur people into action. They'll do anything to avoid it.

A subtle shift in her expression. It's not fear in her eyes. It's uncertainty.

Good. I want her to sit with the sensation that she might have fucked up.

She *has* fucked up, obviously. Caroline could have killed me when I was fourteen, but she didn't. She let me live to suffer until that pain wore away everything but the need for revenge. None of her tricks are going to work. I'm stronger now, in every way possible, and I don't give a fuck about anything.

No.

I give a fuck about one thing.

One person.

Caroline stands in the same spot Haley did when she first came to bargain with me. For a few moments before she sat down, Haley stood on the other side of my desk and tried to disguise her shaking body with a desperate confidence that made me so hard I had to fuck my fist as soon as she went upstairs. She was innocent. She was everything.

The woman standing in her place defiles even the ghosts of her footprints. Caroline, after all, is just like me. The two of us are made of dirt and evil, and Haley is pure and clean and good.

She's the only thing that's good.

She is better off without me.

Grief is a blow to the stomach. I'll never see her again, and she'll be better off. I sent her away before Caroline could find her here. I kept her as safe as I could, which was not very. I kept her with me. I am not safe.

I let the silence go on for another few heartbeats. "I'll dissolve the contract."

"Good." Caroline reaches for her purse. "I'm prepared to sign—"

"Under one condition."

She meets my eyes. "What is it?"

The thing about evil is that it has to be baited. I've spent years circling the Constantines. Years following them and taunting them and prodding them until they finally took the meat in their claws. Caroline has tolerated me fucking with her sons in myriad ways, but I've worn her down. I've made it impossible to ignore this final threat. As wealthy as the Constantines are, they also know that diversification is essential for survival. Real estate can't be the end goal. Time keeps passing, after all. Humans need new technologies. That's where the real money is, not in buildings that will only ever rot.

She's caught in my snare now.

I open the top drawer of my desk and take out the whip.

It's been there for as long as I've owned this house. It's been with me since before the house. I bought it a long time ago.

I bought it to use on Caroline.

They were empty threats, the things I said to Haley. I would never have used this on her. It's not made for kink or safety or sanity. It's meant to leave scars. It's meant to leave wounds. It's meant to make a person bleed.

This is the moment to stand, so I do it. Caroline's eyes follow me up and up and up, and for the first time, they go wide and fearful. I'm taller than she realized. Stronger. Not a fucking teenager that she can groom and use and hurt. And she has made an error. She put herself alone in a room with me.

She tries to sneak a glance toward the door.

"No, Caroline." I punctuate this with exactly the smile she deserves. "You'll leave when I'm finished with you."

I feel nothing but impatience. Nothing. No part of her attracts me. It all disgusts me, repels me. I didn't feel that way with Haley. I felt like a different person. The pain was still there. It will always be there, as long as I live. But she felt it with me. She took it from me, and she cried and begged for more.

Caroline's hand turns to a fist around her purse. "You've turned into a real monster. I should be proud, actually. You're the creature I made."

It's as jarring as a slap, because in this, at least, Caroline is right. I'm the Beast of Bishop's Landing. I'm a fucking animal. Nothing but rage and claws. She made me that way. It's a permanent state.

"Undress."

"Leo," she scolds, as if I've gone distastefully far. I let one fist come down on the desk and lean over it. She backs up a half a step, face pale. "Fine. Okay."

She drops her purse on the ground and starts with the coat. Underneath, she's wearing a sheath dress with a collar made for a younger woman. Her face turns pink when she pulls it over her head. I test the whip against one hand. Caroline notices and moves faster.

Naked, she shivers in my office, and I see the deal she's made with herself. Caroline Constantine is allowing herself to believe that she's chosen this. She believes she's buying her own life back by allowing this punishment.

She's doing no such thing.

I have no interest in enlightening her. I have almost no interest in this woman at all, except in one way. She's had power over me for too long. I want it back.

"There's a coat hook on the back of the door."

Caroline brings her head up and looks at me, questioning. I give her no answers. In the end she has to turn around and walk toward the open office door, then close it. It's set into the center of the wall.

I have never used the coat hook. It was original to the house, and I've always hated it. After Caroline leaves I'm going to rip it out of the door myself.

"Hold on tight."

She sees what I mean and shudders. I could not give less of a fuck. Caroline reaches up for the hook and wraps both hands around it. For all I've loathed it, it's perfect for this one scenario. In order to hold on, Caroline has to be up on tiptoe. It will make the whipping harder to take.

"Let go, and I start over."

Caroline throws a pleading look over her shoulder. "There are other ways to settle things." Veiled panic flickers through her eyes. "Compensation. A—a joint contract involving—"

I interrupt her with the first stroke.

Her head goes back and she screams. The scream itself is slightly delayed while her nerves race to catch up. I draw the whip over the angry red line across her back. "I'm going to say this once." Two taps with the whip. "Shut the fuck up, unless you're going to scream some more."

And Caroline does scream.

By five strokes, she's sobbing. By ten, her screams have gone ragged at the edges. Fifteen and her voice is giving out.

I stop after twenty to give my arm a rest. Her knuckles are white on the coat hook. Her back is red from her neck to her ass. I've landed some blows on her thighs, too. "No more," she whispers. "Please, no more."

The pity I expected to feel doesn't come. I am, after all, a fucking monster. So I don't feel for her, even though I am intimately acquainted with her state of existence.

"Tell me, Caroline." I pace around behind her, letting her hear my footsteps. "Did you go this easy on me?" She starts to shake her head, and I shove the whip in front of her and use it to pull back on her neck. "Tell the truth."

The Constantine ice queen doesn't want to admit it, but after a too-long pause, she opens her mouth. "No. I didn't."

"I believe in fairness." I go back to the other side of her. "It wouldn't be fair to stop now."

I lay down another stripe across her back. Another. Another. Another. So many times I lose count. The screaming is background noise now. The same as the rush of wind outside. I don't hear it, and I don't care about it. The only thing that matters is damaging her. Forever, if possible.

The doctors Eva dragged me to after I came home from Caroline eventually determined that the nerve damage was too extensive to repair, the feedback loop between my brain and the misfiring nerves too deeply carved. They didn't know why. Permanent torture from a whipping that's years over is random, according to medical science. Needless to say, the caliber of painkillers that would fix this aren't compatible with staying alive. Not for a Morelli.

It is unlikely that I can engineer the same outcome for Caroline.

Doesn't mean I can't try.

I bring the whip down three more times. She's hardly making any sound now, and my anger senses weakness. It wants to tear her throat out. It howls at the end of the leash, snapping its jaws. I'm made of aching tension. I want to keep whipping her until she finally crumples, until it's finally over, until she can never hurt me again. I could do it. I'm close. I'm so fucking close.

But then.

What?

If I kill Haley's aunt, she can't come back to me. Not ever. If I kill Caroline Constantine, then it's mutually assured destruction. The family feud will collapse in on itself and explode. It'll take Bishop's Landing and most of New York City with it.

I think of Haley offering her ass up to be strapped, her pussy wet, promising that she would do anything to save her father from me.

I want to kill Caroline.

But I can't kill this foolish hope that I'll see Haley again.

The whip flies out of my hand before I'm aware of the decision to throw it. It clatters against the window and Caroline screams again, a silent, broken thing. "Get the fuck out of my house."

I stalk back to the desk and lean against it to watch. It takes Caroline several tries to let go of the coat hook. Her fingers are probably stiff and sore. Droplets of blood down her back. When she turns, it's with gasping, mincing steps. Caroline can't wander outside with no shirt on. She'll have to cover her wounds with cloth. It'll be horrible to take off.

She grits her teeth and muscles through dressing. The last thing to go on is her coat. Caroline folds her arms over her belly, tucking her purse there. She looks like she wants to say something, but I've taken her voice.

"If you ever come back here, I'll kill you."

Caroline nods. And then she leaves, as fast as her legs will carry her.

CHAPTER TWENTY-THREE

Leo

THE HOUSE SETTLES into silence once Caroline is gone.

I feel her leave, terrified and barely upright. Maybe I imagine it. Not long after her malevolent presence leaves the house, Gerard passes by the door of the office. His footsteps move lightly in the hall. I don't look. Outside, in the courtyard, two robins hop from branch to branch on a gnarled tree. Each time they land, tiny glittering pieces of snow fall to the ground.

I'm watching the birds without leaning back in my chair. One of the simplest things Caroline took from me was the ability to throw myself into any available piece of furniture without thinking, the way my brothers and sisters and other people do. Many times, the pressure of my own body is enough to start a loop, which is how I've come to think of the pain. A circle. A breaking wheel. It intensifies and peaks and lets down again, but it's always, always there. Waiting.

The smaller of the robins hops to the top of the tree. It soars down to the bench nestled near the trunk, then back up.

Hiding the peak of the pain takes up the most time and energy in my life by far. More than arranging extra security for the more trusting of my siblings. More than running my business. More, even, than fucking with the Constantines. Other than Eva, only one person has witnessed it. People have come close. Once, at one of our regular casino nights, Lucian slung his arm around my shoulders so hard I turned the table over. The single convenience, really, is that this particular pain reads as anger. People see what they expect to see.

Make no mistake, I was fucking furious about it for years. Even the Beast of Bishop's Landing can't maintain constant rage, however. Giving myself a stroke wouldn't help the situation unless it killed me.

The bigger bird follows the smaller one up to the high branch, then both of them take flight. They loop around the branch and sail away.

My courtyard is now as empty as I feel. I've spent my entire adult life cultivating my reputation as a fanged beast and exacting revenge. Now

I have it. I'm not much for high expectations but I thought there would be more. More triumph. More relief. A full circle is supposed to give you a sense of completion. I don't sense anything, other than a numb dejection.

Haley didn't shy away from the pain. The initial sight of my skin shocked her. Of course it did. She's a good girl, and good girls like Haley don't live in a world where such fucked-up things happen to people. Her whole heart leaped into her eyes. Not pity. She wanted to understand, and I wanted to let her. I couldn't do it. Not until the night she sat next to me, her hands so careful not to touch anywhere that might hurt me. Haley. Worried about hurting *me*.

She's an impossibility. An oxymoron. A good Constantine shouldn't exist. A good Constantine who looks at me with anything other than terror in her eyes is practically a mythological creature. She begged me not to leave her in that SUV. Tried to follow me out. Tried to stay with me.

In other words, she's a miracle. Godsent. I don't know what joke God thinks he's made, sending her to me. Dangling her in front of me, really, and then snatching her away. I can respect it. It's the kind of cruel bastard thing I would do. Let a person worship at the altar of sweetness, then destroy the altar.

I rub both hands over my face and turn back to the desk. In the most enormous oversight of my life, I didn't make any plans for what I would do after I whipped the haughtiness out of Caroline. There's no to-do list for the aftermath.

Well—there's a short one. I open the wide top drawer of my desk and take out the portfolio that's been resting there since the night Phillip Constantine met me with a heartbreaking hope in his eyes. Inside the portfolio, the contract remains untouched. I take the slim bundle of papers from the inside pocket and flip through them. In a sense, I did the same thing to Phillip Constantine as has happened to me. I teased him with the world and then I took it away.

I lived up to my reputation as a heartless bastard. No one was let down on that account.

The paper goes down without a fight. I tear it into pieces, ripping Phillip's signature in half. This paperwork will never be filed in a way that makes it official or enforceable. I don't do it for Caroline. No. It's Haley's tear-bright eyes I think of. The way she sat up so straight and brave in that empty chair across from me. The way she knew how I was, knew what I could do, and came anyway. She was the virgin sacrifice who offered herself up to the devil. Had she been born in any other time, they would have called her a saint.

Saint Haley would have been the sweetest, filthiest one in history.

I go over to the fire and watch the remains of the contract burn. The corners curl in first, toasting into a pleasant brown before black ash spreads from the center and devours them.

Haley's gone.

I sent her home.

The house feels like a series of shallow breaths. I don't keep a large staff. Mrs. Page and Gerard each supervise their own small teams. Hers include the kitchen and housekeeping, and his include security and grounds management. There are rarely more than twelve people, including myself, on the property at any given time. It's quiet here because that's how I made it.

In Haley's absence, it's more than quiet. It's hollow. Gutted. The fact that she's not in her room or my room or in my den with a book feels like an amputation. Another impossible thing, to lose what I never had in the first place. I'm losing the illusion of having her. The illusion of any kind of grace. I put a hand on the mantel and watch the final shreds of paper combust. It doesn't feel like a fucking illusion. It feels like a metal-tipped whip on already damaged skin.

There's nothing for it.

I go back to the courtyard windows and send a series of mindless emails to the staff in my office. None of their questions make any impression at all. Real estate is a game, and not a particularly interesting one. Its usefulness is mainly in how easy it is to launder money from less savory businesses through shell companies and property purchases. Dirty money in, clean money out. Filter it through a hundred smaller sales that quadruple their money. Repeat. Repeat. Repeat.

The Constantines think they own New York City. I own more of the Constantines than they'll ever realize.

It doesn't matter.

The phone rings in my hand. Not Trenton Alto this time. Another contact. This one is far closer to the Constantines. He looks like one of them. They trust him for it.

"Rick. Good news or bad news?"

The birds have come back to the tree. If Haley was here right now, I might tell her how they are in the early mornings. If you wait on the bench long enough, they'll flutter down and rest in your open palm.

Rick Joseph Jr. clears his throat. "Caroline's

ordered a hit."

The smaller robin flies up to the windowsill and lands on the outer ledge. I put a finger to the glass. It pecks playfully at the window. "Really? On who?"

"You." A long silence. Rick is undoubtedly uncomfortable with it, but I'm not. You have to have feelings to be uncomfortable, and I don't have any at all right now. Only a hollow spot where all my emotions have been whipped away. "Should I…" He's at a loss. Rick isn't the kind of man who takes initiative. He takes opportunities. He takes orders. That's all. "What should I do?"

"Nothing. Do you know who she's sending?"

"The bulldog."

Ronan.

"Fine." I hang up on him. There's nothing more to say.

The motivation to save myself is curiously absent. No point in dragging this out. Ronan will come here, or he'll have to spend the next several days hunting me through the city. All of it would only be a distraction from the fact that I'm dead inside already. Moving the various chess pieces to protect myself would take too much effort to be worth it. I can't even summon the desire to text Lucian, who would at least make things more complicated for Ronan. No. None of my siblings. Save them the angst over the inevitable. Eva can be pissed at me at the graveside.

I put my phone in my pocket and lean both hands on the windowsill. The robin flutters outside. A flare of pain sparks at the base of my spine. The beginning of the loop. Depending on how fast Ronan works, it could be the final one. It makes me feel almost nostalgic for the misery that's coming. If I'm going to die, let the pain do its worst. Death will be a sweet relief.

Forehead against the cool glass, I let it work its way up my spine and across my shoulder blades.

A fine time to have a drink.

I'm in the middle of pouring whiskey into a glass on my desk when Gerard comes into the room.

"Someone will be along to kill me shortly," I tell him. "One of the Constantines' people. If I were you, I'd leave while there's time."

His mouth opens, then closes, the color gone from his skin. "You don't mean that."

"Tell Mrs. Page to pack a bag. She'll need a ride to her sister's. Kitchen and housekeeping, too. No one will have to worry about salary or benefits for a year. They'll be paid out automatically from a trust. Any questions, you can ask Eva."

Gerard shakes his head, speechless.

"I order you to leave, then. I order you to personally clear the staff out of the house and take Mrs. Page to her sister's. Help her pack her suitcase."

"This isn't right."

"Does dying sound right to you?" The first sip of whiskey burns going down. "Don't be fucking foolish, Gerard."

"How is it less foolish for you to die?"

I meet Gerard's eyes and let the silence grow and grow and grow until it's infested every breath of air. "Go now, and don't come back."

Two red splotches have grown on his cheeks. Gerard's not a man who cries. He's unemotional and steady. Even the comings and goings of my sisters don't bother him. But now his eyes have a sheen.

"Oh, for Christ's sake. On balance, the world will be less evil without me in it. Stop pretending otherwise and go."

He nods once, then twice, obviously searching for something to say. Gerard never finds anything. He goes out without another word.

"Gerard," I call.

He pokes his head back in the door.

"Leave the front door unlocked. Every member of the security team goes with you."

He lets out a sharp breath, like I've hit him. Then he really leaves. At first, his footsteps recede at the measured pace he always moves through the housewith. He's still in earshot when he breaks into a run.

My armchair waits for me by the fire. I sit down with the whiskey and watch the flames tangle around each other. A small tapping from the window draws my attention. The robin watches me with black, shining eyes.

"You should leave, too," I say. "It won't be a pretty sight."

The little bird cocks its head to the side. It doesn't believe me, clearly. It waits for a few beats longer and takes to the air on reluctant wings.

I stay where I am and wait to die.

CHAPTER TWENTY-FOUR

Haley

WE'RE SITTING ON the couch in the living room when Ronan takes a call.

I got my dad to eat and sleep last night. I showered. Changed my clothes. Tossed and turned. Couldn't sleep. The morning crawled by. The phone call is the only thing to break up the late afternoon.

My dad stares at the floor, not seeming to notice, but Cash picks up his head from where he's been staring into the fire. We both watch Ronan step toward the front door. "I'm on my way," he says, and then he comes back into the living room at a brisk pace. "No one leaves this house." He points specifically at me. "I'll be back in a few hours. Anyone's gone, and there will be hell to pay."

Ronan leaves before we can answer, slamming the door behind him. A curl of winter wind moves through the living room and ruffles my hair.

"What the fuck was that?" Cash's eyes are pinned to the front door.

I count to three and get up off the couch. Ronan maneuvers his car around in our driveway. The second he's finished he accelerates toward the main road. My heartbeat is lodged in my throat. "This is bad."

"Is it, though?" Cash comes to stand next to me at the window. "He left us alone. That's an improvement."

"He left us alone for what? Ronan's been here because Caroline thinks Dad is the worst threat to the family. They both think he's working for the Morellis. What bigger threat could there be, other than—" My voice dies. The words shrink until they pop out of existence. "Does your car have gas in it?"

"Yeah." Cash glares after Ronan's taillights. "Wait—are you planning to leave? Ronan just said there'd be hell to pay, Hales. We're already in hell. You want to make this worse?"

I'm already grabbing one of Petra's abandoned coats from the last time she lived here and pulling it on. "Where are your keys?" A pair of winter boots are the only footwear in sight, so I put those on too. "Cash. Keys."

"Where are you going?" My dad has chosen to enter the conversation, but he's blinking, confused.

"Stay here, Daddy." I reach into Cash's coat pocket and my fingers meet metal. "You too, Cash."

"No." Cash comes to my side and pulls the coat out of my hands before I can get the keys free. "I'm going with you."

"I'm going to Leo's house."

He meets my eyes, his jaw tight. There isn't time to argue. There isn't time to put together a full presentation on why I am not letting Ronan get to Leo like this. "What the hell happened to you?" Cash pitches his voice low, so Dad can't hear. "He's a Morelli. You should let Ronan kill him. At least then no contract with him would be binding."

"Are you coming or not? Because if you're not, give me the keys and get the fuck out of my way."

Cash blinks first. He shrugs his coat on, cursing under his breath. "I'm driving."

"Great. Let's go." I run back to the couch and bend down to kiss my dad's cheek. "We'll be back soon. Stay here. Stay safe. Don't answer the door." I'm straightening up when he puts his arms around me and pulls me back for a hug.

"I love you, honey."

"I love you too." I swallow unshed tears and follow Cash to the garage. He hefts the door open and backs out. I'm buckled in by the time he's done pulling it closed. "We have to hurry. Please. Go as fast as you can."

It's a good thing Cash is the one at the wheel. My hands shake all the way to Leo's house. I keep thinking we're catching up to Ronan, but every car turns out to be the wrong one. Night is falling by the time Cash steers us down the last long road. There are two tire tracks in pristine snow. No one else has come this way. They also haven't gone. My pulse is out of control.

"Call the police," Cash says, and I do it, barely registering the conversation. I hang up just in time.

"The gate is on the left. Slow down. Slow down. Here."

Cash pulls in, and we both stare up at the stone pillars. The gate is here, technically. It's also swinging open. The locking mechanism has been blown apart. "Okay." Cash nudges the car forward. I hold my breath. The pickets of the gate catch on the front bumper. A little acceleration, and they let us go.

Ronan's car is parked in the circle drive. Cash pulls up behind it. Cold sweat breaks out under my clothes. I could already be too late.

"You're not going in by yourself." He has his neck bent to look up at Leo's house. "That place is a nightmare."

I put a hand on Cash's shoulder, and he straightens up to look me in the eye. "You have to go home now."

"What?" Horror on his face, in his eyes. "What the fuck, Hales? No. I'm not leaving you here with a pair of killers."

"Think about it." I don't want to think about it. "If Ronan finds you here, you're screwed. You know he'll shoot you. He'll shoot anyone who threatens the family image. Dad is alone right now. He can't be alone. I will be okay."

My heartbeat marks the time I'm losing.

"No. No." Cash grips the wheel. "You can't ask me to do this. You—you at least have to wait for the cops to get here."

I pull him into a big, tight hug. "I'm telling you to do it, and you don't have a choice. Go home to Dad and wait for me." I let him go and scramble out of the car, then bang my fist against the window. "Go."

Cash slaps a hand down on the wheel. "Fuck,"

he shouts, but he reaches for the gear shift. I don't have time to watch him leave. I run up the wide stone steps and find the front door cracked open.

"Fuck," I whisper, and go inside.

The silence inside is like death. Like a tomb. It's so deafeningly still that with my breath steadied I can hear voices. They're coming from the hall to the right. That's where Leo's office is. I step out of my boots, abandoning them in the foyer. No wet squeaks to announce my arrival. At the threshold to the hall, I abandon the coat, too. My clothes seem too simple for this moment. Leggings and a long shirt. I should be wearing armor.

Ronan is speaking as I approach Leo's office.

"—blood. There's going to be scarring. She's looking at several reconstructive surgeries."

"Good," Leo answers.

"The balls on you. I always knew Morellis were psychopaths, but whipping Caroline Constantine over a grudge makes you seem terrifying. Or like you have a death wish. Guess it's both."

There's a long, strained silence. During that silence, my pulse jumps into my ears and bangs itself around. The pieces of this puzzle assemble themselves. The older woman. The scars on Leo's back. Caroline. It was Caroline, and I don't have to question it. I know how ruthless she can be. How cold. I've been giving her too much credit. I thought there were lines she wouldn't cross, but Leo was fourteen. I discover I'm holding my hand over my eyes and take it back down. No crying. Clearly, Leo has made things even between them.

Clearly, Ronan is the only one who's meant to know.

"Are you almost done?" Ronan asks. "I've got other jobs today."

I inch myself close enough to see through the door. Ronan's back is to me. He has both feet planted and a gun in one hand. He taps it impatiently against his jeans.

Leo is leaning against his desk.

I breathe in air that feels like knives. No—it's not the air, but the distance between us that's sharp enough to cut. The empty air is a travesty. And Ronan is an abomination. I know I should be watching him, waiting for the right moment to act, but I can't take my eyes off Leo.

He's in the same golden firelight as he was the first night I came here. It draws him in rich color, though his clothes are dark. A black shirt that looks like mine. It's not like mine. I've touched his shirts. They feel so expensive. It's only now, in this horrible moment, that I connect his highly specific wardrobe to something more than money and status. Soft shirts for damaged skin. He can't bear to have anything else touch his scars.

Leo has one foot crossed over the other, his arms folded below his chest, his head bowed. His eyes are closed. Shadows from the firelight cling to his eyelashes. On my next breath, some of the knives pull out. They're replaced by a sensation that feels like a shimmer. Like I'm looking into a church and not into my greatest fear.

A subtle shift in Leo's body. He makes the sign of the cross.

"Fucking finally," says Ronan, and he lifts the gun.

"Stop." I rush into the room between them, conscious with every step that I look ridiculous. I look like nothing. Leo's head snaps up and the shock in his eyes breaks my heart. "Jesus. Stop."

Putting myself between Leo and a man with a gun is not something I've technically rehearsed. I had a vague idea that I would just stand between them, but once I'm headed toward him, I can't stop. I throw my arms around his neck and pull him close. His heart beats so hard I can feel it through my shirt. Leo's hands are on my face, on my hair. He pushes me back so he can look into my eyes.

This close, I can see how blown out his pupils are. I've never felt him tremble before, but it's happening now. Leo Morelli is shaken. Rattled. Like he's seeing a ghost. He expected to be dead already, I realize. He was about to be free of his pain. "What are you doing here?" He crushes me to him and kisses my hair.

"I came to protect you," I say into his shirt. Like my flesh-and-blood body can save him from a bullet to the head.

Leo's breath hitches and he makes room between us, eyes searching my face like it's the last time he'll ever see. "Why? Why?" He swallows. "Why would you do this? I'm the worst kind of person. Why wouldn't you stay where it was safe? I let you go." His teeth click together and he works to unclench them. "I let you go."

Tears come in spite of my best efforts but I refuse to let them fall. "When I look at you, I see someone strong." He's hanging on every word, and it's too much power. The stakes are too high. Too bad. We're here now. "Someone determined. I know—" My voice breaks, god damn it. "I know it hurts. I know it's hard to live with. But don't let her do this to you."

He strokes my hair. "It's already done, darling."

"I believe in you." One tear breaks free of my self-control and runs down my cheek. Leo catches it with his thumb. His eyes go to that silvery droplet like it's a miracle. It was made in pain and love. "And I'm not going to let this happen."

I take Leo's hand and stand beside him, getting as close as I can. Ronan's gun hangs by his side, but impatience twists the corners of his mouth. "That was precious."

"You'll have to kill me too." I'm outside my body already. It's a surprisingly peaceful feeling. I have to die someday. I might as well do it to give this man a fighting chance. "You'll have to kill me first."

Ronan snorts. "Caroline won't be bothered about that much."

Caroline's hitman raises his gun to shoot and I move. What the hell was I doing, standing next to him instead of in front of him? I throw myself in front of Leo and brace for the bullet to hit.

But Leo is faster.

Leo is so much faster.

He wraps one arm around me and uses my own momentum to push me behind him. One step forward. It's so simple. In the space of a single heartbeat, he becomes the human shield.

There's a sound so loud it claps against my eardrums with a painful, insistent pressure. I see that sound wave rock through Leo, feel it pass over my skin. He turns and reaches for me and then we're both falling, falling, falling into the end of the world.

CHAPTER TWENTY-FIVE
Haley

SOMEHOW, I CATCH him.

Or I don't, and there's a mad scramble as he tries to push himself off the floor and fails. I end up on my knees, cradling him in my arms while he twists his body toward me. He's trying to get his back away from the floor but he can't sit up. The best I can do is to hold his head up, hold him close, to take as much of the pressure away as I can.

Leo's dark eyes are wide, the firelight laying bare his crushing pain and shock. I don't dare look away from him. Raindrops fall onto his face. I keep wiping them away with my sleeve.

Raining, inside the house.

Ronan must have shot the roof out, too. But no. No. It's winter, not raining.

It's tears on his face. My tears.

I touch the front of his shirt and find blood there. The bullet hit him in the same place as his stab wound. Blood soaks through the cloth. It doesn't stop.

Hot. It's hot. It's life spilling out of him.

One of Leo's feet kicks and he groans through clenched teeth, twisting himself another inch away from the floor. I'll die if I cause him any more pain. Oh, god.

I was never ready for this. For shifting him, as gently as I can, so that my legs don't dig in. Nothing between us has ever been this intimate.

He has one arm locked around my waist. I have one arm supporting his head and shoulders. His eyes, his eyes. I can't look away. Don't want to. Pain moves through him in a cascade of tensing muscles and Leo makes a sound like a wounded animal.

I've wasted my life. I've wasted my life, studying literature when I could have learned how to save a human being. Now I'm helpless and he's bleeding out. He's dying. He gets a hand up to my face and runs the pad of his thumb over my cheek.

"Christ." His face pales. "Fuck."

"I know. It's going to be okay." It's not. There is so much blood. Leo's eyes slip out of focus and I lean down and kiss him. Too hard. Too hard for a man who's been shot. He grabs my hand in his.

Touches it to his forehead. His chest. One shoulder.

The sign of the cross.

"No. You're going to be okay." I let him finish the movement but I don't want to. It's not time for that yet. He's my own fallen angel; he's going to *live*.

Dimly, I become aware of Ronan. His gun is down by his side, and the sight of him standing there like some sick voyeur fills me with rage.

"Get out," I snap at him. "Either shoot us or get out."

He hesitates, his finger moving toward the trigger. Leo curls into me again and I hold him there until the pain ebbs and he relaxes. I don't know if that's a good thing or if it means he's dying faster. He's been shot. He's going to die. No. Jesus, no.

Ronan hefts his pistol in his hand and looks down at it like it might tell him what to do. Then, with a sigh, he moves it behind his back. A holster under his shirt. I don't care. "If you want to keep him alive, keep him away from Caroline Constantine." He starts to turn away, then stops. "There's nothing left for you in that family."

Leo makes another sound, and there's nothing in the world but him. His eyes are almost black in the light, except for those gold threads. More tears shine on his cheeks. A slow blink. He looks like he's struggling to stay here with me.

"You're okay," I murmur. My instinct is to rock, but moving him would be bad. I just hold him close. More blood pools between us. "You're okay, Leo. It's okay."

His chest heaves with an unholy gasp, and then another one. He must see his panicked eyes reflected in mine, because he tries to make his face look calm. For me. It's for me. "Better with you," he manages, and the next gasp sounds wrong. So very, very wrong.

"It's not better to die with me. That's not happening." I try to smile and fall way short. "I won't let it."

A smile curves up the corner of his mouth. "I was better with you. You—" Leo's starting to sound strangled. Like his lungs can't move enough air. Like they're filling up with blood. "You made me want to become a better man."

The only sound in the room other than the crackle of the fire is the nightmare of Leo struggling to breathe.

"I love—" A cough cuts him off. A deep one. Wet. Blood at the corner of his mouth. I'm falling through the center of the earth and into a black void. I dab at that red stain with my sleeve and put a hand on Leo's face. His eyes are unsteady on mine and then he looks past.

I shake him. I'm not proud of it. I shake his face a little, a desperate sob turning itself inside out in my chest. "Stay here." His eyes come back to mine. "Stay with me. Please."

Another cough. More blood. A wretched gasp, and he squeezes his eyes shut. They open again but it's hard, I can tell it's hard.

"Just hang on. Please, please, please. God, please." I've never been much for prayer. Wouldn't know what to say. But I'll try anything. We haven't had enough time. "Don't go. I'm right here. I'm not leaving."

There's a high-pitched whine in the distance. Shrill. Pained. For a moment I think it's an animal, a wild animal, but then it gets louder. Sirens. They're coming.

Leo's lips move, but no sound comes out. His thumb brushes over my cheek.

A thundering crash shatters the silence of the house, followed by men shouting. I take a huge breath and shout at the top of my lungs. "In here. In here, in here." I can't be more specific. I keep shouting. I won't stop until they save him. They're not going to be too late.

I look down at Leo's perfect face. He's watching me with the trusting confusion of a child.

One more gasp. It hurts to hear it. The footsteps come closer. "In here," I shout again.

Leo's hand falls. Drops, like he has no control over it anymore. The light in his eyes is going out, the fire dimming to embers. I try to gather up his arm. I try my best with my heart tearing, shredding, dying. "In here." My voice breaks. I can't modulate it. Can't get it to work right. "Stay. Stay. Stay." A chant. A plea. A prayer. Two men crowd into the doorway and push through, followed by two more. Panic forces my prayer into a jagged cry rising to a howl.

Leo's eyes close.

The howl turns into raw grief.

And the grief becomes a scream.

✧   ✧   ✧

Thank you for reading SECRET BEAST! We hope you loved Leo Morelli and Haley Constantine's emotional love story. Find out what happens next in **HIDDEN BEAUTY**.

Haley Constantine traded her life for her father's safety. Now she's trapped in a castle with the Beast of Bishop's Landing.

Her own family wants her dead.

The only man who can save her is the one she can't trust.

Dangerous. Tortured. Furious. Leo Morelli wears a mask of cruelty to cover up a lifetime's worth of scars. He's been injured, but that only makes him fight harder. The only thing he cares about more than revenge is the woman he's come to love.

One click HIDDEN BEAUTY on Amazon, Barnes & Noble, Apple Books, Kobo and Google Play.

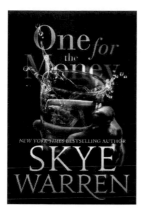

And you can read Eva Morelli's angsty and swoony love story now!

Finn Hughes knows about secrets. His family is as wealthy as the Rockefellers. And as powerful as the Kennedys. He runs the billion-dollar corporation. No one knows that he has a ticking time clock on his ability to lead.

Eva Morelli is the oldest daughter. The responsible one. The caring one. The one who doesn't have time for her own interests.

Especially not her interest in the charismatic, mysterious Finn Hughes.

A fake relationship is the answer to both their problems.

One click ONE FOR THE MONEY on Amazon, Barnes & Noble, Apple Books, Kobo and Google Play.

And you can read Ronan's love story right now!

The flare of a cigarette and the handsome Irishman in the shadows—I wanted it all, but I wasn't allowed to want. Ronan was danger and beauty, murder and mercy. To me, he was a mystery, but he was also the only man who ever knew me.

You can find STOLEN HEARTS on Amazon, Barnes & Noble, Apple Books, Kobo and Google Play now.

The warring Morelli and Constantine families have enough bad blood to fill an ocean, and their brand new stories will be told by your favorite dangerous romance authors. See what books are available now and sign up to get notified about new releases here…

www.dangerouspress.com

ABOUT THE AUTHOR

Amelia Wilde is a *USA TODAY* bestselling author of steamy contemporary romance and loves it a little *too* much. She lives in Michigan with her husband and daughters. She spends most of her time typing furiously on an iPad and appreciating the natural splendor of her home state from where she likes it best: inside.

For more books by Amelia Wilde, visit her online at https://awilderomance.com.

About Midnight Dynasty

Midnight Dynasty is a brand new world where enemies and lovers are often one and the same.

JOIN THE FACEBOOK GROUP HERE
www.dangerouspress.com/facebook

FOLLOW US ON INSTAGRAM
www.instagram.com/dangerouspress

SIGN UP FOR THE NEWSLETTER
www.dangerouspress.com

COPYRIGHT

This is a work of fiction. Any resemblance to actual persons, living or dead, business establishments, events or locales is entirely coincidental. All rights reserved. Except for use in a review, the reproduction or use of this work in any part is forbidden without the express written permission of the author.

Secret Beast © 2021 by Amelia Wilde
Print Edition

Published by Dangerous Press